JEAN PIERRE LABAGUETTE AND THE NARCO PRESIDENT.

Richard T Clement

Table of Contents

PROLOGUE (1)

(1) from the Book Jean Pierre Labaguette for US President

Jean Pierre Labaguette, once a celebrated restaurateur in New York, built a culinary empire alongside his wife, Sylvie, and their twin children. His charm and culinary prowess not only won over his patrons but also members of the Republican Party. Seduced by his charisma, they invited him to join their ranks, and with no suitable candidates for the presidency, Jean Pierre found himself propelled to the highest office in the land.

Born in the United States and raised in France driven by Sylvie's relentless ambition, Jean Pierre secured the presidency. However, his tenure was plagued by controversial decisions, growing unpopularity, and a sex scandal. Multiple attempts on his life underscored the chaos of his administration, and an orchestrated political disgrace led Congress and his own party to seek his impeachment. Confined to house arrest in the White House, his world unraveled further.

Sylvie betrayed him, engaging in an outrageous affair with the pool boy and embracing vegetarianism, a sharp departure from the meat-centric empire they had built. To make matters worse, the Haitian White House chef Fete Nationale, once a loyal ally, turned against Jean Pierre, blackmailing him and seizing control of his beloved restaurants.

Fleeing disgrace, Jean Pierre escaped to France by boat, where an unexpected reunion awaited him. His estranged twin brother, once the proprietor of a classic French bistro, had reinvented himself, running a kebab shop and converting to Islam.

Despite being pursued by Interpol and facing prosecution in the United States, Jean Pierre fought to clear his name and secure a presidential pardon. While his legal battles raged on, he returned to his roots, opening a new restaurant in France, a modest endeavor that rekindled his love for cooking and his belief in second chances.

01 | BACK TO THE USA

Jean-Pierre Labaguette had always been a man of tradition. His restaurant, Chez Labaguette, nestled in the heart of Lyon, was once a haven for gastronomes seeking the essence of French culinary art. With its rustic decor, recipes passed down through generations, and the aroma of freshly baked bread mingling with garlic and thyme, it was everything Jean-Pierre loved about his homeland.

Jean-Pierre Labaguette's hands worked the dough with practiced precision, folding and stretching it against the cool marble countertop. The kitchen of Chez Labaguette smelled of butter and freshly milled flour, with faint undertones of thyme and garlic from the day's preparation. Yet, for all its comforting familiarity, the act felt mechanical.

His gaze drifted to the window. Outside, Lyon's cobblestone streets were bathed in the muted light of a gray November morning. Years ago, he had felt pride seeing the bustle of diners streaming into his restaurant. Now, the streets were dotted with the garish signs of fast-food chains, their blinking neon mocking the charm of the old brasseries they had replaced.

"Is this what we've become?" he muttered, shaking his head.

Jean-Pierre's return to France had been bittersweet from the start. When Jean-Pierre Labaguette left the United States, he didn't just leave behind a scandal—he abandoned a legacy. His name, once revered in the elite culinary circles of New York, became synonymous with controversy. He had built an empire, transforming his small bistro into a Michelin-starred institution frequented by politicians, celebrities, and high society. But the same ambition that had fueled his rise had also led to his downfall.

Hasty deals. Unsigned contracts. A financial empire that grew faster than he could control. The cracks widened until they could no longer be ignored. Accusations turned into federal investigations. Whispers became headlines. The grand illusion collapsed.

The courtrooms had been his final stage, a place where his fate was no longer in his hands. The judge's expression was unreadable, but Jean-Pierre knew what was coming. His lawyer had laid out the reality—prison was inevitable. That was when Jean-Pierre made the most calculated decision of his life. He wouldn't stay to watch his empire burn. He wouldn't wait for the final judgment.

He vanished under the cover of darkness. He traveled from Washington to Cancun, then by sea to Dunkerque, and finally by train to Lyon, France— hoping to escape the scandals and start anew in a city where food was revered. At first, it worked. Chez Labaguette, his restaurant, gained recognition for its bold French flavors and traditional cuisine. But no matter how many dishes he perfected, no matter how many satisfied customers walked through his doors, one truth remained:

Jean-Pierre Labaguette was never meant to live in exile. His mind was still in America, where real power awaited.

At first, exile had been a blessing. In Lyon, he reclaimed the simplicity of cooking for the sake of the craft. Chez Labaguette became a sanctuary where he could lose himself in the rhythm of the kitchen. But France had changed in his absence, and Jean-Pierre soon found himself at odds with a world that seemed to value convenience over quality.

Fast-food chains multiplied like weeds, their processed menus replacing the seasonal dishes Jean-Pierre cherished. Diners no longer lingered over meals, savoring each bite; instead, they ate quickly, their attention split between their plates and their phones. Even at Chez Labaguette, the pressure to adapt was relentless.

Jean-Pierre glanced at a menu pinned to the wall, the original offerings from the day Chez Labaguette first opened. Coq au vin, ratatouille, tarte Tatin—it was a snapshot of a time when French cuisine was revered.

Now, even his restaurant wasn't immune to change. Requests for gluten-free this and vegan that became common. He had removed pork from his tarte flambée to accommodate new religious dietary preferences, a change that felt like a betrayal of everything he stood for.

"This is not cooking," he muttered, slamming the dough onto the countertop. "This is survival."

It wasn't just the food that had changed. The France Jean-Pierre had returned to felt foreign in other ways too. Taxes on small businesses like his were crushing, a labyrinth of bureaucracy that seemed designed to choke the life out of entrepreneurs. Each month, Jean-Pierre pored over incomprehensible forms, watching his hard-earned euros disappear into the government's coffers.

"It's hopeless," he said one evening, staring out at the nearly empty dining room. By the next morning, the staff at Chez Labaguette were abuzz with news of a bold move. Jean-Pierre had announced a new menu: "L'Âme de la France"_"The Soul of France."

The dishes were unapologetically traditional, prepared with techniques honed over decades: coq au vin, cassoulet, ratatouille, and his legendary tarte Tatin. Each plate was a defiant reminder of what French cuisine could—and should—be.

"This is what it means to be French," Jean-Pierre declared to his patrons that evening, standing at the center of the dining room. His voice carried over the soft clinking of cutlery. "To respect the seasons, to savor each bite, and to take pride in our culinary heritage."

Some diners applauded; others exchanged skeptical glances. The next day, the backlash began. Social media buzzed with divided opinions. Supporters hailed him as a guardian of tradition, while critics dismissed him as an outdated relic.

Jean-Pierre read one scathing review in the local paper: "Labaguette is clinging to a past that no longer exists." He folded the paper neatly and placed it on the table.

"Perhaps it no longer exists here," he said to himself. "But elsewhere... perhaps it does."

The announcement of Jean-Pierre's pardon sent shockwaves across the world. The news broke from the White House, where President Donald Trump in a surprising political maneuver, signed the executive pardon that erased Jean-Pierre's legal troubles. Officially, the pardon cited "contributions to the culinary and cultural landscape of the United States" as justification. Unofficially, insiders speculated it was a strategic move—one designed to win favor with the growing base of Francophiles, culinary elites, and international allies who had long advocated for Jean-Pierre's return.

Reactions were swift and divided. His supporters hailed the decision as a recognition of his unparalleled influence in the culinary world. "Jean-Pierre Labaguette is more than a chef," a renowned food critic declared on a late-night talk show. "He is a symbol of tradition, excellence, and resilience—a man who represents the kind of brilliance America should embrace, not exile."

Critics, however, saw the pardon as yet another example of political favoritism, a move that let a disgraced mogul walk free while others faced the full force of the law. But regardless of public opinion, one thing was certain—Jean-Pierre Labaguette was no longer an exile. He was free. "What kind of message does this send?" a panelist on a 24-hour news network fumed. "That you can run from justice as long as you make a good steak?"

Social media erupted with hashtags like #JusticeForJean and #FoodNotFraud, sparking heated debates in every corner of the internet. Memes circulated, contrasting Jean-Pierre's face with exaggerated headlines like "From Fugitive to Foodie" and "Make America Taste Again."

For Jean-Pierre, the pardon was neither a victory nor a scandal. It was a lifeline. A second chance.

The news reached Jean-Pierre one quiet morning at Chez Labaguette. He was tasting a batch of his signature tarte Tatin when the television buzzed with breaking news.

"I'm issuing this pardon to one of the greatest culinary artists of our time," Donald Trump's voice boomed across the screen. The footage cut to Trump standing confidently at a podium, flanked by aides. "Jean-Pierre Labaguette is a genius. His steak au poivre ? Unbelievable. His tarte Tatin? Life-changing. America deserves the best, and that's what we're bringing back."

Jean-Pierre froze, fork halfway to his mouth. His staff stopped what they were doing, their eyes glued to the screen.

"Labaguette represents excellence," Trump continued. "And you know me—I only want the best. This is about tradition. This is about greatness. And it's time to bring it home."

Jean-Pierre set the fork down slowly, his appetite replaced by a swirl of emotions: confusion, disbelief, and the faintest flicker of hope.

One of his waiters leaned closer, whispering, "Chef... does this mean you can go back?"

Jean-Pierre didn't answer. His mind raced as he processed the weight of the announcement.

In the following days, the world's reaction was swift and polarizing. His restaurant in Lyon became the epicenter of media attention. Reporters gathered outside the doors, desperate for a comment.

Jean-Pierre avoided them, retreating to the solace of his kitchen. His staff, however, buzzed with speculation.

"Chef," his sous chef began cautiously during a quiet moment, "are you... considering it? Going back to America?" "I understand Your ex-wife and twin children are still living in America "

Jean-Pierre stirred a pot of bisque, his movements deliberate. "I don't know," he admitted. "Returning means facing everything I ran from. It means opening old wounds."

"But it also means starting fresh," the sous chef said, his tone hopeful.

Jean-Pierre didn't respond.

The letter arrived a week later, delivered by a sharply dressed envoy from the U.S. embassy.

Jean-Pierre opened the envelope slowly, his hands trembling. The letter bore the presidential seal and read:

"Dear Jean-Pierre,

Your pardon is official. Welcome back to the land of opportunity! Time to reignite your legacy and make culinary history together.

Yours truly,

Donald J. Trump"

Jean-Pierre reread the letter twice, his emotions a conflicted tangle. The pardon was real, and with it came the chance to reclaim everything he had lost. But it also meant returning to a city that had watched him fall from grace.

A few nights later, Jean-Pierre sat in the quiet dining room of Chez Labaguette, sipping a glass of

Burgundy and staring at the framed menu from the restaurant's opening day.

"What do I even say to them?" he murmured to himself. "To my children? To Sylvie?"

Marc, his oldest friend and former maître d', walked in and sat across from

"You say the truth," Marc said simply.

Jean-Pierre chuckled bitterly. "And what is that, exactly? That I ran because I was afraid? That I left them to deal with the fallout?"

Marc shrugged. "Or that you're ready to come back. To rebuild. To do what you do best."

Jean-Pierre swirled the wine in his glass thoughtfully. "You make it sound so simple."

Marc leaned back, a faint smile on his lips. "It's not simple, my friend. But it's necessary."

A FEW WEEKS LATER AT JFK AIRPORT

"Jean-Pierre!" Donald Trump's booming voice broke through the chaos of the Photographers. The former president strode toward him, flanked by security. "Welcome back to America!"

Jean-Pierre forced a smile. "Monsieur Trump, this welcome is... overwhelming."

"Overwhelming? You're gonna love it. Big plans, Jean-Pierre. Huge plans.

. We're reopening your restaurant, Chez Labaguette, right here in Manhattan."

Jean-Pierre's brow furrowed. "Chez Labaguette? In Manhattan?"

"Exactly! Same name, same tradition, but with that American flair. It's what the people want," Trump said, guiding him toward a waiting limousine.

"American flair?" Jean-Pierre muttered as he climbed inside.

Trump grinned. "Trust me." "You will no longer be an apprentice"

Two weeks later, Chez Labaguette reopened in the heart of Manhattan's Upper West Side. The restaurant's facade retained its rustic charm, with wooden shutters and a painted sign that read Chez Labaguette—A Taste of France.

Inside, Jean-Pierre moved through the kitchen like a conductor leading an orchestra. He tasted sauces, adjusted seasoning, and barked orders in a mix of French and English.

"Where is the beurre blanc?" he demanded, waving a ladle.

A young chef rushed forward with a pan. "Here, Chef!"

"Too thin," Jean-Pierre snapped, tasting it. "Add more butter. This is not soup!"

The dining room was packed with patrons, many of them high-profile guests invited by Trump. A waiter approached Jean-Pierre nervously.

"Chef, Mr. Trump would like to see you at his table," he said.

Jean-Pierre sighed. "Of course, he does."

In the corner, Trump sat with a group of guests, gesturing enthusiastically as he regaled them with stories.

"Jean-Pierre! There you are," Trump said as the chef approached. "Ladies and gentlemen, the genius behind tonight's meal."

Jean-Pierre gave a slight bow. "I hope everything is to your satisfaction."

"Satisfaction? This is the best steak au poivre I've ever had," Trump declared.

A woman at the table chimed in. "Chef, your tarte Tatin is extraordinary. It's like tasting Paris itself."

Jean-Pierre smiled, his first genuine smile of the evening. "Merci. It is good to see people appreciate tradition."

After the last table was cleared and the kitchen was spotless, Jean-Pierre stepped outside into the cool night air. He leaned against the building, staring at the city lights.

The sound of footsteps pulled him from his thoughts. A teenage boy stood a few feet away, his hands shoved into his pockets.

"Patrick?" Jean-Pierre said, his voice barely above a whisper.

The boy nodded. "Hi, Papa."

Jean-Pierre's heart raced as he stepped closer. "How long have you been here?"

"A while," Patrick replied. "I wanted to see if you'd really come back."

Jean-Pierre reached out, placing a hand on his son's shoulder. "I have. For good this time."

The boy's face softened, but before he could respond, another voice called out from the shadows.

"Patrick, don't hug him all to yourself."

Jean-Pierre turned to see Jacqueline, his daughter, walking toward them with a broad smile.

"Jacqueline," he said, his voice cracking as she wrapped her arms around him.

"You look terrible," she teased, pulling back to study his face.

"And you look beautiful," he replied, his eyes misting.

From behind them, a third figure emerged.

"Are we just going to stand in the street all night?" Sylvie said, crossing her arms.

Jean-Pierre froze. "Sylvie..."

She approached him slowly, her expression unreadable. "You have a lot of explaining to do."

"I know," he said softly., "You have a lot of explaining to do also"

Sylvie glanced at the restaurant behind him, then back at her family. "But for now, let's go inside. It smells like home."

02 | THE TRIP TO THE CARIBBEAN

After the whirlwind of reopening Chez Labaguette and reconnecting with his family, Jean-Pierre knew it was time for something different. His family had been through so much, and despite their newfound closeness, he could sense the need for a change of pace—a chance to step away from the restaurant, the city, and the lingering shadows of their past.

"It's time to enjoy life," Jean-Pierre declared one late evening as the family gathered in the kitchen. He placed a stack of travel brochures on the table, their glossy covers showing exotic destinations: golden deserts, snowy mountains, and sunlit beaches.

Patrick was the first to grab a brochure. "Safari in Africa? We'd need mosquito nets and hats. Pass."

Jacqueline flipped through one showcasing the wine country of Argentina. "This looks nice. Vineyards, rolling hills, and food! Oh, and they do tango!" She twirled dramatically, nearly knocking over a glass of water.

Jean-Pierre smiled. "Little less choreography, I will never be able to dance tango?"

Sylvie picked up a brochure featuring the Caribbean. The cover showed a sailboat gliding across turquoise waters with a white sandy beach in the background. "What about this? A week at sea, sun, beaches, and seafood. Jean, you'd love it."

Jean-Pierre studied the image. "Sailing? Hmm. Only if someone else does the work."

Jacqueline grinned. "It says here the boat comes with a skipper, two private cabins, and a fully equipped kitchen."

Patrick shrugged. "Fine by me. Just no lectures about butter sauces, Papa."

Jean-Pierre raised his hands in mock surrender. "Then it's settled. The Caribbean it is."

TOUCHING DOWN IN PARADISE

The Labaguettes landed in St. Maarten two weeks later. The humid air wrapped around them like a warm embrace as they stepped onto the tarmac. Jean-Pierre adjusted his hat and squinted at the tropical scenery.

"This is... different," he muttered, wiping a bead of sweat from his brow.

"It's beautiful," Sylvie said, her voice softer than usual, her gaze sweeping over the lush greenery and the turquoise sea sparkling in the distance.

Jacqueline pulled out her phone, holding it high to capture the perfect shot. "This lighting is everything. I'm tagging this 'Island Goals.'"

The car ride to Anse Marcel Marina was equally picturesque. Narrow roads wove through emerald hills, offering glimpses of colorful villas perched high above the coastline. Each turn revealed breathtaking views—sparkling bays, tiny roadside markets, and fields of wildflowers swaying in the breeze.

Jean-Pierre stared out the window, momentarily captivated. "It's charming," he admitted, though his brow furrowed as he added, "but where are the bakeries?"

Jacqueline rolled her eyes. "Papa, not everything is about bread."

When they arrived at the marina, their sailboat awaited them: "The Privilege". Its sleek design and polished teak deck glistened in the sunlight, exuding sophistication.

Standing beside the boat was their skipper, Larry.

Sylvie's breath caught the moment she saw him. He was tall and broad-shouldered, with bronzed skin that glowed under the Caribbean sun. His white linen shirt was casually unbuttoned at the collar, hinting at a muscular chest, and his shorts revealed strong, athletic legs. His dark hair was tousled just enough to suggest a man who spent his life outdoors, but it was his easy, confident smile that struck her most—it was the kind of smile that made you want to linger, to trust him without question.

"Welcome aboard!" Larry called out, his deep, velvety voice cutting through the warm air like a melody.

Jean-Pierre approached first, his posture stiff with his characteristic reserve. "Jean-Pierre Labaguette. My family and I look forward to this... adventure."

Larry extended a hand, his grip firm and assured. "Pleasure to meet you, Chef. I've heard a lot about you."

Jean-Pierre raised an eyebrow. "I'm sure you have."

But Sylvie barely registered the exchange. Her eyes were fixed on Larry as if drawn by some magnetic pull. The way he stood, effortlessly commanding yet approachable, made her stomach flutter.

When Larry turned his attention to her, his gaze met hers with a spark that sent a subtle warmth coursing through her. She smiled, her lips parting slightly as if words had momentarily escaped her.

"I'm Sylvie," she said, her voice lower, softer than she intended. "And these are our twins, Jacqueline and Patrick."

Larry held her gaze for a second longer than necessary, his own smile widening as he gestured toward the boat. "Let's get you all settled. This week is going to be unforgettable."

As Larry stepped ahead, leading the way to the sailboat, Sylvie adjusted her hair, her cheeks now faintly flushed. Her gaze lingered on his broad back, the way his movements seemed effortless yet deliberate.

Jacqueline nudged her mother with a knowing smirk. "Enjoying the view, Mom?"

Sylvie cleared her throat, glancing away quickly. "It's... quite a boat."

Jacqueline chuckled, clearly unconvinced.

Jean-Pierre, entirely oblivious, studied the gleaming deck of the sailboat as they stepped aboard. But Sylvie found her mind wandering, drawn back to the warmth of Larry's smile and the quiet confidence he carried like a second skin.

DAYS OF SUN AND SEA

The first morning aboard "The Privilege" was magical. The family awoke to the gentle rocking of the boat and the sound of waves lapping against the hull. Patrick and Jacqueline were the first on deck, marveling at the endless expanse of turquoise water stretching to the horizon.

"Can we snorkel today?" Jacques asked, his excitement barely contained.

"Creole Rock is perfect for that," Larry replied as he adjusted the sails. "It's a coral reef teeming with fish. You'll love it."

Jean-Pierre watched Larry's ease at the helm with a mix of admiration and suspicion. "You seem to know these waters well."

Larry grinned. "Been sailing them for over a decade. They're like a wet playground."

The snorkeling excursion didn't disappoint. Patrick and Jacqueline dive into the clear water, their laughter echoing as they explored the vibrant coral reef. Sylvie stayed on deck, sipping a cold drink and occasionally glancing at Larry as he worked.

Jean-Pierre spent the afternoon spearfishing with Larry. Despite himself, he was impressed by the skipper's skill and knowledge of the sea.

"Not bad," Larry said as Jean-Pierre expertly speared a snapper.

Jean-Pierre smirked. "Precision is key in both cooking and fishing."

That evening, they grilled their catch on the beach, the scent of butter and garlic wafting through the air. Jean-Pierre couldn't help but take charge, instructing everyone on how to prepare the sides.

"This," he said, holding up a perfectly grilled lobster tail, "is why fresh ingredients matter."

Larry chuckled. "You're passionate, Chef. I respect that."

Jean-Pierre nodded but said nothing, choosing to focus on the meal.

STROLLING THROUGH SERENITY

One evening, the family ventured onto a secluded beach after dinner. The setting sun bathed the sky in hues of orange and gold, casting long shadows over the pristine sand.

"This place is magical," Sylvie said, walking barefoot beside Jean-Pierre.

"It's certainly... peaceful," he admitted, though his tone carried a hint of reluctance.

Jacqueline pointed to a group of tourists waddling toward the water, their sunburns glowing bright red. "Look at them! They're like walking lobsters!"

Jacqueline burst out laughing, and even Jean-Pierre allowed himself a rare chuckle.

Larry, who had joined them, smirked. "Do you enjoy the quiet, Chef?"

Jean-Pierre nodded. "I do. It's a welcome change."

Larry gestured to the tourists. "Until they show up."

The group laughed, the tension between Larry and Jean-Pierre easing, at least for the moment.

A NIGHT UNDER THE STARS

Their final evening aboard "The Privilege" was one they would never forget. Jean-Pierre, determined to make it special, prepared a lavish meal featuring their freshly caught fish, tropical fruit salads, and Sylvie's favorite dessert: a light, airy coconut soufflé.

As they dined on deck, the sky above them transformed into a canvas of stars. The sound of waves gently lapping against the boat provided a soothing backdrop to their conversation.

"To family," Jean-Pierre said, raising his glass.

"To new beginnings," Sylvie added, her voice tinged with emotion.

As if on cue, fireworks from a nearby celebration lit up the horizon, their vibrant colors reflecting on the water. Patrick and Jacqueline gasped in delight; their faces illuminated by the bursts of light.

For Jean-Pierre, it was a moment of clarity. This trip had been more than just a vacation. It was a reminder of life's simple joys, the power of connection, and the importance of stepping away from the familiar to rediscover oneself.

03 | THE CHRISTMAS PRESENT

T he night sky over the Caribbean was ablaze with fireworks, their golden and crimson bursts scattering across the heavens like celestial blooms. The gentle rocking of "The Privilege "added to the surreal magic of the evening, its polished deck glowing under the flickering lights.

Jean-Pierre stood at the bow; his usually furrowed brow softened as he gazed upward. The vibrant display reflected in his eyes, a rare moment of tranquility washing over him.

"Look at that one!" Patrick shouted, pointing as a cascade of golden sparks erupted into the shape of a star before fizzling into nothingness.

"Magnifique," Sylvie murmured, her voice barely audible over the distant booms. Her gaze lingered on the horizon, where the last hues of sunset had surrendered to the deep blues of twilight.

Jacqueline, perched on the railing, had her phone raised high, capturing the scene. "This is so much better than Times Square!" she declared, her enthusiasm infectious.

Jean-Pierre chuckled, turning slightly. "That's because you're not packed in with a million other people like sardines, my dear."

The family burst into laughter, their joy rising with the crescendo of the fireworks. The warm Caribbean air carried the scent of salt and hibiscus, wrapping around them like an embrace. It was a perfect moment, the kind that Jean-Pierre wished could last forever.

But the universe had other plans.

A new sound began to creep into the night, faint at first but growing steadily louder. It wasn't the crackling of fireworks or the rhythmic lap of waves against the hull. It was something unnatural, mechanical—a deep, rumbling sound.

Jean-Pierre's contentment evaporated as he frowned and shielded his eyes, scanning the darkened sky. "What's that?" he asked, his voice cutting through the family's excitement.

Sylvie straightened, her brows knitting together. "It sounds like... an engine?"

The noise grew closer, a guttural roar that made the deck vibrate under their feet. Patrick and Jacqueline exchanged uneasy glances.

Larry emerged from the cabin; his expression already cautious. "It's flying too low," he muttered, his gaze locking onto a faint blinking light in the distance.

As the noise intensified, a small airplane came into view, its outline barely discernible against the night sky. It circled the area once, its movements erratic, before banking sharply. The plane's lights blinked with unsettling regularity as it descended further, flying at a height that made even Larry uneasy.

"What's it doing?" Jacqueline asked, gripping the railing.

Larry's jaw tightened. "Something it shouldn't be."

The plane dropped lower still, its engine now a deafening roar. Then, without warning, large, dark objects parachuted from its cargo hold, plummeting into the water below with loud splashes.

"Are they... dropping supplies?" Patrick asked, his voice tinged with doubt.

"Not the kind you want," Larry muttered under his breath.

The family watched in stunned silence as the plane circled again, releasing more bags into the sea. The splashes echoed ominously in the still night, the ripples spreading like tiny shockwaves.

Then, as if fate had decided to escalate matters, one of the bags veered off course. It tumbled through the air, spinning wildly before crashing onto the deck of "The Privilege" with a sickening thud.

Sylvie screamed, stumbling backward as the heavy bag mere feet from where she had been standing. Jean-Pierre instinctively reached for her, his hand steadying her as her breathing quickened.

Larry moved swiftly; his movements purposeful. "Stay back!" he barked, his tone leaving no room for argument.

The deck of "The Privilege" seemed to hold its breath as Larry crouched over the mysterious bag and his parachute. His fingers worked quickly, unfastening the straps with a practiced efficiency that hinted at familiarity with such situations.

"What is it?" Jean-Pierre asked, stepping forward despite Larry's warning.

"Jean, let him handle it," Sylvie said, her voice trembling.

But Jean-Pierre's curiosity won out. He approached cautiously, his eyes narrowing as Larry opened the bag.

The skipper froze for a moment, his hands hovering over the contents. Slowly, he pulled out a tightly wrapped package. The dim light caught on the plastic covering, which was sealed with thick, industrial tape.

Larry's expression darkened, his shoulders tensing. "It's cocaine," he said grimly, his voice barely above a whisper.

The words hit the family like a physical blow. Jacqueline gasped, her hand flying to her mouth as she stumbled backward. Patrick's wide eyes locked onto the package; disbelief etched across his face.

Sylvie gripped the railing, her knuckles turning white. "Cocaine?" she repeated, as if saying it aloud would make it less real.

Larry nodded, setting the package back into the bag. "A lot of it," he added, his tone flat but heavy with meaning.

Jean-Pierre took a step back, his mind racing. This was not the kind of drama he had envisioned when they embarked on their Caribbean escape.

The hum of engines grew louder, slicing through the silence like a blade. Jean-Pierre's heart pounded in rhythm with the sound as the speedboat emerged from the darkness. Its sleek black hull glistened under the faint moonlight, and its headlights glared with an intensity that felt deliberate, like the eyes of a predator locking onto its prey.

"They're coming for it," Larry's voice low and urgent. His eyes flicked toward the horizon, narrowing at the faint outline of a speedboat closing in fast. He turned sharply to Jean-Pierre. "Take the bag. Hide it in the galley. Now."

Jean-Pierre froze, the weight of the moment pressing down on him. His mind raced with questions. Who are they? How did they find us? But Larry's tone brooked no argument.

"Go!" Larry barked, snapping Jean-Pierre out of his daze.

Grabbing the bag, Jean-Pierre was struck by its surprising weight. It felt heavier than he thought, its, foreboding contents making his chest tighten. With adrenaline surging through his veins, he scrambled below deck, nearly tripping on the narrow stairs.

The galley was cramped and dimly lit, the faint scent of saltwater and stale bread lingering in the air. Jean-Pierre yanked open a storage compartment near the sink, his fingers fumbling with the latch.

"Come on," he muttered under his breath, his pulse pounding in his ears.

The door creaked open, and he shoved the bag inside, wedging it between an old kettle and a stack of tins. He slammed the door shut, securing the latch with trembling hands. For a moment, he just stood there, staring at the closed compartment, his breathing shallow.

The enormity of what he'd just done hit him like a tidal wave. He wasn't just complicit; he was actively hiding evidence—evidence that could cost him his freedom or worse.

"Get back up here!" Larry's voice echoed down the stairs, sharp and commanding.

Jean-Pierre wiped his damp palms on his trousers, took a steadying breath, and climbed back up to the deck.

Above deck, Larry's silhouette was a wall of defense against the encroaching threat. The speedboat came to an abrupt stop alongside "The Privilege", its engine idling menacingly.

A Latin man with a Colombian accent stood at the bow radiated authority. His tailored white shirt, unbuttoned just enough to reveal a glinting large gold chain, seemed out of place on the open sea. Yet his eyes, sharp and unrelenting, made it clear that he was not to be trifled with.

"¡Oye!" he barked, his voice carrying easily across the water. "Did you pick up a bag? It belongs to me!"

Larry took a single step forward, his frame blocking the man's view of the family. His stance was steady, his tone calm. "We've seen nothing," he said, his words clipped and deliberate.

The man's lips curled into a sneer, his dark eyes narrowing as he scanned the deck. "Don't lie to me, amigo," he said, his accent thick, every syllable carrying a threat. "My men saw it fall onto your boat."

41

Sylvie, clutching to Patrick, leaned toward her son. "Who is he?" she whispered, her voice barely audible.

"You do not know me? My name is Pedro Musk Obar from Antioquia Colombia" Pedro asked, his lips curling into a humorless smile. He gestured toward himself with exaggerated flair. "I am Musk Obar. Surely, you've heard of me. The name landed like a stone in the pit of Jean-Pierre's stomach.

Pedro laughed, the sound harsh and clipped. "No? Then you are either very stupid or very lucky, Niño." He turned to his crew, who were already leaning over the side of the speedboat, using poles and nets to fish the remaining packages from the water.

Pedro's smile vanished. "You speak as though you have a choice."

"These bags," Pedro continued, his voice growing colder, "are worth more than your entire life." He took a step forward, the deck creaking beneath his weight. "I suggest you don't pretend ignorance when dealing with me."

Larry remained unfazed, his hand resting near the holster of his handgun. "This is private property," he said, his voice low but firm. "Whatever you're doing here, it's not our concern. Take your bags and leave." "Patron, we've got most of them," one of the men called out.

Pedro didn't turn. His eyes remained locked on Larry, sizing him up like a predator assessing its prey. "Most," he repeated, the word laced with dissatisfaction.

He stepped closer to the railing of "The Privilege", his movements deliberate. "If there is one bag missing," he said, his tone icy, "I will find it."

Larry didn't flinch. "You won't find it here."

Pedro raised an eyebrow, his expression both amused and threatening. "We'll see about that."

Jacqueline, who was standing near his father whispered to him "What do we do if they come aboard?"

Jean-Pierre's voice was steady, though his hands trembled. "They won't. Larry won't let them."

From behind Larry, Jean-Pierre silently prayed that would hold true.

Pedro turned his attention back to Larry, his expression now one of mock civility. "You are brave, gringo. Or foolish. Both tend to end the same way when you cross me."

Larry met his gaze, his tone unyielding. "You're not crossing this boat. Take your men and your bags and go."

Pedro studied him for a moment, then laughed softly. "You think you can scare me? I have built my empire on fear, amigo. Fear is my currency."

Pedro gestured sharply, and three men in the speedboat sprang into action. They moved with precision, their rifles slung casually over their shoulders but ready to be used at a moment's notice.

"Ve y compruébalo," Pedro ordered, his voice icy.

The men began to board The Privilege, their boots thudding ominously against the deck.

Patrick says to Larry looking at the thugs" you told us no shoes on deck "

"Stay where you are!" Larry's voice rang out, sharp and commanding. In one swift motion, he pulled a handgun from his waistband and aimed it directly at the advancing men.

The Narcos froze, their eyes flickering between Larry and Pedro, waiting for their leader's signal.

Pedro's expression darkened. "You're outnumbered, gringo," he sneered. "Stand down, and we'll take what's ours. No one has to get hurt."

"This is private property," Larry repeated, his tone unyielding. His grip on the handgun was firm, his finger resting just shy of the trigger. "You're not setting foot on my boat."

The tension was suffocating. The family, huddled near the cabin, watched with wide, fearful eyes. The air was thick with the unspoken promise of violence, every breath a calculated risk.

Just when the situation seemed poised to erupt, another sound cut through the night. The deep, powerful hum of a larger engine grew closer, accompanied by the sweeping beams of searchlights.

"Patrón! ¡La guardia costera!" said one of the men that wanted to step on the boat.

Pedro's head snapped toward the source of the noise, his jaw tightening. His expression shifted from confident to furious as the unmistakable silhouette of a coast guard patrol boat came into view.

"Patrón, la guardia costera" one of his men repeated.

Pedro cursed under his breath, his glare snapping back to Larry. "You are lucky tonight," he spat. "But this isn't over. Those bags belong to me, and I will get them back."

He raised a hand, signaling his men to retreat. They moved quickly, jumping back onto the speedboat. The vessel roared to life, its powerful engines sending a spray of water into the air as it sped away into the darkness.

The family remained frozen, their breaths shallow as the sound of the speedboat faded. Larry lowered his gun but didn't holster it, his eyes scanning the horizon for any sign of the returning threat.

Sylvie was the first to break the silence. "What... what just happened?"

Larry shook his head, his voice barely above a whisper. "That was Pedro Muskcobar."

Jean-Pierre emerged cautiously from behind, his face pale. "Are they gone?"

"For now," Larry replied, his tone grim. He glanced toward the approaching patrol boat, its lights now fully illuminating "The Privilege". "But this isn't over."

The speedboat disappeared into the darkness, its engines fading into a faint hum that was soon swallowed by the vastness of the sea. In its wake, the waters churned frothily, the only sign of the chaos that had just unfolded.

Moments later, the coast guard vessel pulled up alongside "The Privilege", its imposing frame dwarfing the sailboat. Searchlights swept over the deck, making the Labaguettes squint against the brightness. The sharp metallic smell of fuel mixed with the salty air as armed officers positioned themselves along the patrol boat's railing, their weapons gleaming under the lights.

An officer at the bow, dressed in a bulletproof vest and helmet, leaned forward, his machine gun slung across his chest. His voice was sharp and commanding as it carried over the gentle lapping of waves. "Where did they go?"

Patrick, his heart pounding, stepped forward despite the terror knotting his stomach. He pointed shakily toward the fleeing speedboat, his voice steadier than he felt. "That way," he said.

The officer gave a curt nod and turned to his crew, motioning them forward. The patrol boat's engines roared back to life, sending plumes of water cascading behind it as it sped into the night.

Jean-Pierre exhaled a breath he hadn't realized he'd been holding. "They're gone," he muttered, his voice barely audible.

"For now," Larry replied, his eyes narrowing as he watched the patrol boat disappear into the distance.

A HEAVY BURDEN

Below deck, the atmosphere was thick with tension. The galley, once a haven for laughter and shared meals, now felt oppressive. The bag sat in the center of the table, a dark and unyielding presence that seemed to dominate the room.

Jean-Pierre paced the small space, his hands running through his hair. His normally composed demeanor was frayed, his mind racing with possibilities and dangers.

"What do we do now?" he asked, his voice strained.

Larry leaned against the wall; arms crossed. His face was drawn, the usual spark in his eyes replaced with grim determination. "We can't keep it," he said. "But we can't leave it here, either. If Pedro Muskcobar finds out we have his cocaine..."

Sylvie, seated at the corner of the table, wrapped her arms tightly around herself. "We have to tell the authorities," she said, her voice trembling. "This isn't something we can handle on our own."

Larry shook his head. "Not yet. The coast guard is chasing the Narcos now, but if they come back and find this, we're in trouble. They'll assume we're involved."

Jacqueline, sitting beside her mother, looked at Larry with wide eyes. "But we're not criminals. They'd believe us, wouldn't they?"

Larry's gaze softened slightly as he looked at her. "Maybe. But you don't want to rely on 'maybe' when it comes to situations like this."

Patrick broke the silence, turning to his father. "What do you think, Papa?" he asked, his voice quiet but insistent.

Jean-Pierre stopped pacing and looked at his son, his expression a mixture of frustration and helplessness. For years, he had thrived on precision, control, and predictability in his life and career. Now, he was adrift in a situation he couldn't have anticipated.

"I think," he began slowly, choosing his words carefully, "that we must be very careful. This is no ordinary Christmas gift."

Jacqueline bit her lip, glancing at the bag. "It's more like a curse," she murmured.

Sylvie reached out, placing a hand on Jean-Pierre's arm. "We can't pretend this didn't happen. If Pedro comes back—"

"He won't come back," Larry interrupted, his tone firm. "Not tonight, at least. He's spooked, and the coast guard is all over the area. But that doesn't mean we're safe."

Jean-Pierre sighed, rubbing his temples. "Then what do we do? We can't keep this... poison. But we can't just throw it overboard and hope it disappears".

Patrick frowned, his gaze shifting between his father and Larry. "What if we handed it over anonymously? Left it somewhere for the authorities to find?"

Larry shook his head. "Too risky. It could trace back to us."

The room fell silent again, the weight of their predicament pressing down on them.

Finally, Jean-Pierre straightened, his expression resolute. "For now, we keep it hidden. Tomorrow, we'll figure out the next step. But whatever we do, we must stay calm. Panicking will only make things worse."

Larry nodded, though the lines of worry etched into his face remained. "Agreed. But be ready for anything. Pedro Muskcobar isn't the type to let something like this slide."

Sylvie shivered, pulling her shawl tighter around her shoulders. "It's like something out of a nightmare."

Jean-Pierre placed a hand on her shoulder, his touch both comforting and reassuring. "We'll get through this," he said, though the words felt hollow even to him.

As the family filed out of the galley, leaving the bag behind, Larry lingered for a moment, his gaze fixed on the ominous package.

"You are trouble," he muttered under his breath before turning off the light and following the others above deck.

04 | THE SCENARIOS

The following morning, the tension in the galley was suffocating, pressing down on everyone like an unseen weight. The small room, which had once been with laughter and the comforting aroma of freshly prepared meals, now felt alien and hostile. At the center of it all sat the bag of cocaine, a dark and unyielding presence that seemed to draw all eyes toward it.

Patrick broke the silence first, unable to contain his curiosity. His voice cut through the oppressive quiet like a spark in dry air. "How much is it worth?"

Jean-Pierre's head snapped toward his son, his expression a mixture of disbelief and anger. "Ten years in jail," he snapped, his voice sharp and unwavering. "Or a bullet between the eyes." He paused, his gaze flicking briefly toward the bag before landing back on Patrick. "Yes, Patrick, it's worth a lot of money."

Patrick flinched at the intensity of his father's tone but didn't look away. Across the table, Jacqueline leaned slightly toward her brother, her lips parted as though about to speak, but she said nothing. Her eyes, however, betrayed a flicker of excitement she couldn't suppress.

Larry, leaning casually against the counter, seemed unfazed by the gravity of the situation. If anything, he appeared amused, as though the whole ordeal were some thrilling adventures rather than a life-threatening predicament.

"I want my share," Larry said, his tone light but deliberate. His lips curled into a smirk as he crossed his arms. "With it, I'll buy a bigger boat. Something fast, sleek—perfect for these waters."

The twins' faces lit up at Larry's words, their imaginations taking flight. Jacqueline turned to Patrick, her voice brimming with enthusiasm. "We could open a restaurant in St. Martin!" she said, her eyes sparkling. "Imagine it—a little French bistro by the beach in Grand case. People would love it!"

Jean-Pierre slammed his palm on the table, the sharp sound cutting through the room like a whip. Everyone jumped, their eyes snapping to him.

"No way," he said, his voice rising with barely controlled anger. "This is not a game! We can't just... keep it." He pointed at the bag as if it were a live grenade. "We have to give it back to Muskcobar. It's too dangerous."

"You're stupid!" Sylvie's voice was sharp and biting, her cheeks flushed with anger. She stepped forward, her hands clenched into fists at her sides. "This is a lifetime opportunity, Jean-Pierre! Do you even realize how much this could change everything for us?"

Jean-Pierre's jaw tightened, his nostrils flaring as he turned to face her. "Opportunity? To get killed?" His voice cracked under the strain of his emotions, betraying the fear he tried so hard to suppress. "Is that what you want for our family?"

Larry pushed off the counter, his movements smooth and deliberate. He stepped closer to the table, his presence commanding. "Listen," he began, his tone calm and measured. He rested his hands on the edge of the table, his gaze steady as he addressed the group. "We split it. Equal parts. Everyone gets what they want. I get my boat, the kids get their restaurant, and you..." He turned to Jean-Pierre with a slight shrug. "Well, you can do whatever you need to do."

Jean-Pierre opened his mouth to argue, but Sylvie cut him off. She moved to Larry's side, her hand resting lightly on his knee as she leaned in slightly. "Yes," she said, her voice softening, taking on an almost conspiratorial tone. "Let's split it. I can help you get that bigger boat with my share."

Jean-Pierre's eyes darkened, his frustration bubbling into anger. "Not again!" he shouted, rising to his feet so abruptly that his chair scraped loudly against the floor. "You left me for a pool boy when we lived in America and now a skipper? You seem to have a fascination for water."

Sylvie's lips curled into a smirk, her voice dripping with mockery. "And muscular men," she shot back, her words like daggers. "Face it, Jean-Pierre, you're a French looser over the hill. A little man. I want my freedom—and my share."

The room fell into stunned silence. Even Larry, who had maintained his composure throughout, shifted uncomfortably. His gaze flickered toward Jean-Pierre, as if gauging how far the man could be pushed before breaking.

Patrick cleared his throat hesitantly, his voice barely above a whisper. "Papa..."

Jean-Pierre held up a hand, silencing his son. His chest rose and fell heavily as he fought to regain control of his emotions. After a long moment, he exhaled slowly, his shoulders sagging under the weight of the moment.

"Fine," he said finally, his voice heavy with resignation. "Do what you want. But don't come crying to me when this all goes wrong."

A BITTER DEPARTURE

The morning sun cast a soft golden glow over the marina, its warmth in stark contrast to the icy tension lingering aboard "The Privilege". The Labaguettes moved silently, each burdened by their own thoughts as they prepared to disembark. The atmosphere was thick, weighed down by the unspoken truths and fractured relationships that had emerged in the wake of the previous night's arguments.

Jean-Pierre stood at the edge of the deck, watching as Patrick and Jacqueline shuffled down the gangplank, their heads bowed and their bags clutched tightly. He wanted to reach out to them, to say something that would bridge the growing gap between them, but the words refused to come.

Sylvie's laughter drifted across the water, light and carefree, but to Jean-Pierre, it sounded like a taunt. She leaned casually against the cabin doorway, her hand resting on Larry's arm as she whispered something that made him grin.

Jean-Pierre turned back, his eyes narrowing as they locked onto hers. "Big mistake," he said, his voice low and flat, each word laced with warning. "You're going to end up in jail."

Sylvie tilted her head, her expression unreadable. "I'm not giving back the cocaine," she replied smoothly, her tone as calm as the sea around them.

He shook his head, the weight of disbelief and sorrow pressing heavily on his shoulders. There was nothing left to say, no fight left in him to argue. As he turned and began to walk away, his steps were slow, deliberate. Each movement felt like dragging a chain behind him, the burden of his fractured world refusing to relent.

He didn't look back, even as Sylvie's laughter floated after him, mingling with the gentle lapping of the waves.

AFTERMATH

Jean-Pierre trudged down the dock, the early morning light casting long, uneven shadows across the worn planks. The salty breeze tugged at his coat, but it did little to lift his spirits. His grip tightened on the leather bag hanging at his side, its weight feeling impossibly heavy. It wasn't just the physical burden of the bag that weighed on him—it was the culmination of everything it represented: betrayal, loss, and the disintegration of the life he had so carefully built.

His mind was a maelstrom of unanswered questions. Why had Sylvie stayed? Was her decision driven by loyalty to Larry, or had she truly convinced herself that she could handle the situation on her own? And what of Patrick and Jacqueline? Were they complicit in this madness, or simply innocent bystanders swept up in the chaos of adult choices they couldn't fully understand?

Jean-Pierre clenched his jaw, his emotions surging in turbulent waves. Anger, despair, and regret fought for dominance, each one more suffocating than the last.

"This wasn't supposed to be my life," he thought bitterly, the words echoing in his mind like a mantra. He had envisioned something better, something more stable—not just for himself, but for his family.

Each creak of the gangplank beneath his feet felt like a judgment, a reminder of the dangerous cargo hidden in the inconspicuous bag slung over his shoulder.

Patrick and Jacqueline walked ahead; their steps unusually heavy for teenagers usually bursting with energy. Jean-Pierre watched them, his heart twisting. They are his teenagers, his responsibility, yet here they were, involved in something so far removed from the life he had tried to build for them. Were they complicit in this madness, or simply swept up in its unrelenting tide?

Jacqueline adjusted the strap of her bag, her face a careful mask of indifference. Patrick kept his head down, avoiding his father's gaze. The sight of their silent compliance weighed heavily on Jean-Pierre. He wanted to say something, anything to bring them back to reality, but no words came.

Behind him, the sound of laughter drifted across the still water. Jean-Pierre turned, his jaw tightening as he spotted Sylvie on the deck of the boat. She leaned casually against Larry, her hand resting on his arm as they exchanged easy smiles. To anyone else, it might have looked like a picture of carefree camaraderie, but to Jean-Pierre, it was a betrayal that cut deep.

He stopped and turned fully, his gaze locking onto Sylvie's. "This is a mistake," he said flatly, his voice low but firm.

Sylvie met his eyes, her expression unflinching. "Maybe," she replied, tilting her head slightly. "Or maybe I'm finally doing what's best for me."

05 | THE MULE

The morning was deceptively serene, the marina bathed in soft sunlight that sparkled on the water's surface. The gentle lapping of waves against the hull of "The Privilege "seemed to mock the tension that simmered on board.

A DESPERATE VISIT TO THE "OFFICE DES DOUANES"

The police station was unassuming, its peeling paint and the faded sign reading "Office des Douanes" giving it an air of neglect. Jean-Pierre stood outside for a moment, his breath shallow, his palms damp with sweat. The bag slung over his shoulder felt heavier with every passing second, its contents a silent accusation.

He stepped toward the door, each footfall feeling like a march toward judgment. The creak of the hinges echoed in the quiet as he pushed it open, stepping into a dimly lit room that smelled faintly of stale coffee and disinfectant.

Behind the desk sat an officer, a black man in his fifties. His stern face framed by the kind of exhaustion that came from years of chasing problems that only seemed to multiply. He looked up, his expression shifting from boredom to mild curiosity as Jean-Pierre approached.

"I need to report something," Jean-Pierre said, his voice trembling despite his best efforts to sound composed.

The officer raised a weathered eyebrow. "What kind of 'something'?"

Jean-Pierre hesitated, his fingers tightening around the strap of the bag. With a deep breath, he placed it on the counter, the sound of its weight landing on the wood reverberating through the room. "It's... drugs," he admitted, his voice barely above a whisper. "Cocaine. A lot of it."

For a moment, the officer didn't react, as though he hadn't fully processed the statement. Then, his face twisted in incredulity. "You brought it here?" he asked, his voice rising slightly, the disbelief evident.

"I didn't know what else to do," Jean-Pierre stammered, his hands clenching at his sides. "I thought"

"You thought bringing it here would solve your problem?" the officer interrupted, throwing his hands up in exasperation. His voice carried the weight of countless frustrations. "Do you have any idea how much cocaine we already have stored? We are burning it and it keeps coming".

Jean-Pierre flinched, the officer's outburst hitting him like a physical blow. "I want just to leave it," he protested weakly. "It's dangerous!" "It belongs to a Pedro Muskcobar and he is after us"

"Dangerous?" The officer leaned forward, his voice dropping to a sharp, cutting whisper. His eyes bore into Jean-Pierre's with an intensity that made him take an involuntary step back. "You think you've made it less dangerous by bringing it here? Muskcobar doesn't forget, my friend. If he finds out you've crossed him, you're as good as dead. And now you've dragged us into your mess!"

Jean-Pierre's lips parted, a protest forming on the tip of his tongue, but the officer raised a hand, silencing him with a gesture. "Here's what you're going to do," the officer said, his tone cold and unyielding. "Take it back to where it came from. Or better yet, Take it back to Muskcobar in Colombia and deal with it there."

THE PERILOUS JOURNEY

Jean-Pierre's journey began with a flight to Panama City. The bustling airport was alive with the sound of holiday travelers—families exchanging cheerful chatter, children squealing with excitement, and announcements echoing over the intercom. The festive atmosphere clashed with the storm raging in his mind.

He clutched the bag tightly, his knuckles white against the worn leather strap. The thought of its contents sent a shiver down his spine. Every step felt heavier, every passing glance a potential threat.

As he approached the customs line, Jean-Pierre's eyes were drawn to one officer in particular. The man was a dead ringer for Santa Claus. He was stout, his broad shoulders filling out the white uniform jacket that strained slightly at the buttons. A thick, snowy white beard spilled over his chest, and his rosy cheeks gave him a warm, almost jovial appearance.

But it was his eyes that held Jean-Pierre's attention—twinkling blue orbs peeking out from behind rounded wire-frame glasses, sparkling with an unsettling mix of authority and mischief. The officer leaned forward slightly, resting his hands on the counter, his gloved fingers tapping a steady rhythm that felt almost too casual for someone in his position.

"Step right up, son," the officer called, his deep, velvety voice carrying a faint jolliness that made Jean-Pierre's stomach tighten.

Santa Claus in customs? Jean-Pierre thought, his nerves flaring. The absurdity of the image almost made him laugh, but the weight of the bag in his hand was enough to keep him grounded.

As Jean-Pierre approached, the officer's piercing gaze swept over him, taking in every detail with unnerving precision. "What do we have here?" the man asked, gesturing to the bag.

Jean-Pierre forced a smile. "Just personal items. Clothes. Books."

The officer raised a bushy eyebrow, his expression equal parts amused and skeptical. "Books, huh? Let's take a look." As he was ready to open the bag, his dog barked at another passenger. He shifted his attention to the other passenger.

He unzipped the other passenger bag with deliberate slowness pulling out a French cheese.

He kicked the dog "You stupid dog" "Go ahead all of you I really hate my job!!! Cheese, cheese ridiculous" "both of you go."

"Merci," Jean-Pierre whispered, his voice barely audible as he took the bag, stepped and winked at the dog.

THE BOGOTÁ ENCOUNTER

Arriving in Bogotá, Jean-Pierre was immediately struck by the stark contrast. The airport was less festive, its atmosphere one of quiet efficiency and visible security. Armed guards patrolled the terminal with sharp eyes, their presence a constant reminder of the region's struggles with crime and narcotics.

Jean-Pierre kept his head down, his movements deliberate and unhurried. He couldn't afford to attract attention. But as he reached customs, his luck ran out.

The officer inspecting his bag paused, his expression shifting from routine boredom to sharp focus. Slowly, he unzipped the bag, revealing the tightly wrapped packages inside.

"Señor," the officer said, his voice a mixture of curiosity and disbelief as he held up one of the packages. "Cocaine?"

Jean-Pierre's stomach churned. His mouth went dry as he tried to form a response, but no words came.

Three officers gathered around the bag, their expressions a mix of incredulity and amusement.

"A gringo bringing cocaine into Colombia?" one of them muttered, shaking his head.

"This is a first," another agreed, smirking.

"Maybe he got on the wrong plane," the third joked, drawing laughter from his colleagues.

Jean-Pierre was escorted into a small, sterile office, the weight of his predicament sinking in with every step. Sitting behind a desk was the head of customs—a middle-aged man with sharp eyes and an air of quiet authority.

The man gestured for Jean-Pierre to sit. "Why bring cocaine to Colombia, my friend?" he asked, his voice calm but probing.

Jean-Pierre hesitated before recounting the entire story. His voice trembled as he spoke of Muskcobar's threats, the arguments with his family, and his desperate attempt to do the right thing.

The boss listened intently, his sharp eyes never leaving Jean-Pierre. When the story was finished, he leaned back in his chair, rubbing his chin thoughtfully.

"You're on a dangerous journey," he said finally, his tone tinged with both warning and pity. "Our jails are not... user-friendly. And Muskcobar? He's astute. And violent."

"I know," Jean-Pierre replied, his head dropping into his hands. The gravity of his situation felt unbearable.

THE BOSS'S PLAN

Outside the office, the customs officers gathered, their expressions a mix of confusion and disbelief.

"A gringo smuggling cocaine?" one said, his tone skeptical. "This has to be a setup."

"Or maybe he's a journalist," another suggested, rubbing his chin.

The boss stepped out, silencing their murmurs with a sharp glance. "Let him go," he said firmly.

The officers exchanged incredulous glances. "But why?" one asked, his voice tinged with disbelief.

"Because he'll lead us to Muskcobar," the boss replied. "Place a GPS tracker in his luggage. Have agents follow him. We'll use him to get to the bigger fish."

Inside the office, Jean-Pierre sat stiffly, his thoughts racing. The boss returned; his demeanor suddenly friendlier. He handed Jean-Pierre a business card with a tight smile.

"Go to Medellín," he said. "Find Muskcobar. And when you do, call me."

Jean-Pierre stared at the card, his hands trembling. "You're letting me go?"

The boss's smile widened. "We trust you, my friend. Tell Muskcobar, we say hello. Hasta luego."

Jean-Pierre left the office, the weight of the drugs pressing down on him like an anvil. As he walked through the terminal, he felt the invisible eyes of agents tracking his every move.

Booking a flight to Medellin for the following day and a Hotel in Bogota for the night. This was no longer about doing the right thing. It was about survival and the odds were stacked against him.

06 | LOOKING FOR MUSKCOBAR

Jean-Pierre leaned against the window of his modest hotel room; his gaze fixed on the lively streets of Usaquén below. The cobblestones were alive with activity—vendors shouting to passersby, stalls brimming with colorful wares, and street musicians strumming guitars under strings of soft golden lights.

"Charming," he muttered to himself, gripping the strap of his bag. But the vibrant energy of the district couldn't quell the storm in his mind.

Inside the bag lay the cause of his troubles: cocaine, pure and dangerous. Its presence weighed on him like a millstone.

"I need to get rid of this cocaine," he murmured, his voice barely audible. "Find Muskcobar, settle this nightmare, and get back to my kitchen. Back to my life."

He turned away from the window, the image of "Chez Labaguette" flashing in his mind. The hum of conversations, the clatter of pans, the aroma of fresh-baked bread—it all felt like a lifetime ago.

SEARCHING FOR MUSKCOBAR

Determined to act, Jean-Pierre descended into the bustling streets, the bag pressed tightly against his side. He approached a jewelry stall, the glint of silver and gemstones catching his eye.

"Señor," he began, his voice low. "Do you know Pedro Muskcobar?"

The vendor's smile vanished instantly. Without a word, he turned away, busying himself with rearranging his wares.

Jean-Pierre tried again at a nearby stall selling woven bags. "Pedro Muskcobar?"

The woman froze, her expression turning to fear. She quickly crossed herself, muttering a prayer under her breath. "Go away," she whispered, grabbing her child's hand and retreating into the safety of her shop.

Jean-Pierre sighed heavily. "A ghost," he muttered. "The man might as well not exist."

RESTLESS NIGHTS

Back in his hotel room, the thin walls offered no respite. Outside, Bogotá's nightlife thrived—car horns blared, stray dogs barked, and distant laughter carried through the warm night air.

Jean-Pierre paced the room, the unopened bag sitting heavily on the bed. He couldn't bring himself to unzip it, as though seeing its contents might make the danger more real.

"Every plan falls apart," he muttered, running a hand through his hair. "Every road lead to nowhere."

Through the window, he saw a group of teenagers on the curb, passing around a guitar. Their carefree laughter made his chest ache with longing for simpler times.

"I need answers," he said, grabbing his jacket. "Now."

A DESPERATE NIGHT

Jean-Pierre stepped out into the humid night air, flagging down a taxi with a sharp wave. The cab screeched to a halt, its driver rolling down the window.

"Where to, amigo?" the man asked, smoke curling from the cigarette tucked in the corner of his mouth.

"Take me to the nightlife district," Jean-Pierre replied curtly.

The driver smirked knowingly. "Plenty of chicas there. 1/3 DEA agents, 1/3 drunk tourists agents 1/3 narcos, you'll have a good time."

Jean-Pierre's eyes narrowed. "I'm not looking for chicas. I need to find a man named Pedro Muskcobar."

The name landed like a grenade. The driver's smirk vanished, replaced by a look of alarm. He slammed on the brakes and pulled over abruptly.

"Get out," he barked, his tone sharp.

"What?" Jean-Pierre frowned. "Why?"

"You're looking for trouble. Muskcobar is dangerous," the driver snapped. "I don't know him, and I don't want to know him. Out. Now."

Jean-Pierre hesitated, but the man's glare left no room for negotiation. He climbed out, the bag's weight biting into his shoulder.

As the taxi sped away, its taillights fading into the distance, Jean-Pierre turned to notice a glowing neon sign above a nearby nightclub called

"Papasitos.", the red letters pulsing in time with the salsa music spilling out onto the street.

THE NIGHTCLUB

Inside, the club was a kaleidoscope of color and sound. Couples spun gracefully on the dance floor; their movements perfectly synchronized to the pounding salsa beat. Laughter and conversation mingled with the music, creating an intoxicating atmosphere.

Jean-Pierre edged toward the bar, his eyes scanning the room. Muskcobar could be anywhere—or nowhere. Either way, this was his best chance.

"What can I get you?" the bartender asked, leaning over the counter.

Jean-Pierre hesitated. "I'm looking for someone," he said, lowering his voice. "Pedro Muskcobar."

The bartender's expression flickered briefly before returning to neutral.

Before he could respond, two hands covered Jean-Pierre's eyes, he could smell a strong perfume and a soft voice purred in his ear. "¿Quién es? Guess who I am, amigo."

Jean-Pierre stiffened, the warmth of her touch setting him on edge. "I... I don't know," he stammered.

Her laughter was low and teasing. "I'll give you a hint. We've met before in a Jacuzzi in France, you escaped from jail.

Jean-Pierre turned, and the memory of the sex scandal hit him instantly. She was beautiful—dark hair cascading like silk, crimson lips curling into a knowing smile.

"I remember the sex tapes" he said cautiously. "But that was my twin brother Pierre Jean, not me."

"Convenient," she said, arching a brow. "And hard to believe."

Jean-Pierre shifted uncomfortably; her sharp gaze locked on him. The club's noise seemed to fade as the tension between them grew.

"Trust me," he said, his voice measured, "I'm not the man you think I am."

Her crimson lips curved into a sly smile. "Oh, really? Then who are you, mon cher?"

"Jean-Pierre Labaguette," he replied, extending a hand with polite formality.

She ignored it, leaning closer instead. "Labaguette? That's rich. You were the cook turned US president the brother from America what a surprise?"

A soft laugh escaped him despite the situation. "And you, mademoiselle? What should I call you?"

"Call me whatever you like, as long as you buy me a drink, I am Sandra" She gestured to the bartender, "two arguadientes"

Jean-Pierre hesitated before nodding to the bartender, who quickly poured the drinks.

As she sipped her drink, she studied him with curiosity. "So, Jean-Pierre," she began, her voice dripping with amusement. "Why are you here? And don't tell me it's for the music."

"I'm looking for someone," he admitted, his voice low.

"Let me guess." She leaned forward; her tone conspiratorial. "Pedro Muskcobar."

Jean-Pierre's brow furrowed. "How do you know that?"

She laughed again, a sound that seemed equal parts amusement and warning. "Darling, everyone knows Muskcobar. And everybody in Bogota know you are looking for him, why are you looking for him?"

Jean-Pierre hesitated, then decided there was no point in lying. "I have... business with him."

Her eyes sparkled with mischief. "Business? Or trouble?"

"Both," he admitted.

They moved to a corner table near the edge of the dance floor, the hum of the club providing a strange kind of privacy. Jean-Pierre placed the bag at his feet, but her eyes flicked to it immediately.

"What's in the bag?" she asked, her voice light but her expression serious.

"Something Muskcobar would be very interested in," he replied vaguely.

She arched a brow. "Mysterious. I like it."

He leaned forward, his voice firm. "Do you know where I can find him?"

Her gaze didn't waver. "Maybe. But Muskcobar doesn't meet with just anyone. He likes people to earn his attention."

"And how do I do that?" Jean-Pierre asked.

Her lips twitched into a smirk. "Let's start with why you're really here."

Jean-Pierre sighed, running a hand through his hair. "I'm trying to fix a mistake. A big one. And Muskcobar is the only person who can help me."

Her expression softened slightly. "You're in over your head, aren't you?"

"Way over," he admitted.

She swirled her glass of Arguadiente thoughtfully. "You're either very brave or very stupid.""Probably both."

THE FIRST KISS

Their banter turned lighter as the drinks flowed. She laughed at his dry humor, her hand occasionally brushing his across the table. The chemistry between them was undeniable, a magnetic pull that grew stronger with each passing moment.

"So, Jean-Pierre," she said, her tone playful. "What would your brother think of you now?"

He smirked. "He'd probably say I'm making the same mistakes he did."

"And are you?" she asked, leaning closer.

"Not yet," he replied, his voice softening.

Their eyes met, and for a moment, the noise of the club faded into the background. Her lips curled into a faint smile before she leaned in, her breath warm against his cheek.

"Let's make a mistake together," she whispered.

Jean-Pierre didn't hesitate. Their lips met in a slow, deliberate kiss, the kind that carried both passion and promise. Her hands slipped around his neck, pulling him closer, and he responded with equal intensity.

When they finally pulled apart, her eyes sparkled with mischief. "You're not as innocent as you pretend to be, Jean-Pierre."

"And you're more dangerous than you look," he countered.

She laughed, grabbing his hand and pulling him toward the door. "Come on, gringo. Let's see if your bravery holds up outside this club."

A DANGEROUS DRIVE

The humid night air wrapped around them as they stepped out of the club. The neon lights of Parque de la 93 reflected off the rain-slicked streets, casting shifting patterns of red and yellow.

Jean-Pierre raised a hand, signaling a cab. Within moments, a battered yellow taxi screeched to a halt beside them.

"You're quick," she teased, brushing her fingers against his arm.

"Only when it matters," he replied with a faint smile, opening the door for her.

She slid into the back seat gracefully, her dress catching the light as she settled in. Jean-Pierre followed, closing the door with a firm click.

The driver, an older man with weathered skin and deep-set eyes, glanced at them in the rearview mirror. A cigarette dangled from his lips, the smoke curling lazily toward the cracked window.

"Where to, amigos?" the driver asked, his voice raspy.

Jean-Pierre hesitated, his instincts sharpening. "Hotel Santa Fe," he said cautiously.

The driver nodded and shifted into gear, the cab lurching forward.

As the city blurred outside the windows, she leaned in close, her breath warm against Jean-Pierre's ear. "Take a picture of the driver," she whispered.

Jean-Pierre frowned, turning his head slightly. "Why?"

Her tone remained light, but her eyes held a seriousness that made his pulse quicken. "Just in case," she said. "If we get kidnapped, it might help."

He stared at her, his nerves prickling. "Kidnapped? Is that a possibility?"

She shrugged with a smirk. "Not likely. But with Muskcobar 's name on your lips, who knows?"

Jean-Pierre sighed, pulling out his phone. He angled it discreetly toward the driver, snapping a photo as the man muttered something under his breath about nosy tourists.

"Happy now?" he asked, sliding the phone back into his pocket.

"Very." She smiled, leaning back against the seat, "Send it to your lawyer".

The car sped through the city, its headlights cutting through the dark. Jean-Pierre couldn't help but glance at her from the corner of his eye. She exuded a calm confidence, her posture relaxed as if they were on an ordinary ride home. Her dress shimmered faintly in the passing light, and the corners of her lips curled into a knowing smile.

"You don't seem worried," he said finally.

She turned to him, her dark eyes glinting. "Worried about what? The driver? Muskcobar? Or you?"

"All of it," Jean-Pierre admitted.

Her laugh was soft, almost comforting. She reached over, placing a hand on his knee. "Relax, gringo. If anything goes wrong, just tell them you're with me."

"And that'll work?"

"It's worked before," she said with a wink.

Jean-Pierre wasn't entirely convinced, but her confidence was infectious. For the first time in days, he allowed himself to breathe a little easier.

A NIGHT OF PASSION

The door clicked shut behind them, and she turned, her gaze locking onto his. The air between them was heavy with tension, anticipation crackling like static.

"Jean-Pierre," she teased, stepping closer, "are you going to keep staring at me, or are you going to do something about it?"

He smirked, shrugging off her dress and letting it drop to the floor. "Maybe I'm just enjoying the view."

"Flattering," she murmured, brushing a finger against his chest. "But I think you can do better."

"Better than flattering?" he asked, catching her hand and holding it between them.

Her voice dropped, low and inviting. "Better than your brother, maybe."

He froze for a second, the jab hitting home. Then he laughed softly, leaning in close. "Let's not bring him into this."

She grinned, pulling him closer until their lips met. The kiss was a slow burn, deliberate yet urgent, her hands slipping into his hair as his found the curve of her waist.

They stumbled toward the bed, her laughter ringing softly in the room.

WHISPERS IN THE DARK

"Speak to me," she whispered, her voice breathless and accented.

"In French?" he teased, his lips brushing her collarbone.

She let out a soft laugh, her hands pulling him closer. "Oui... Je veux ça."

He obliged, his voice low and rough. "Tu es belle... fascinante... parfaite," he murmured against her skin.

Her response was immediate, a soft moan escaping her lips. "Encore," she demanded, her accent thick. "Don't stop."

He smiled against her neck, his hands tracing her form. "As you wish, chérie."

Her voice rose as she responded in a mix of French and Spanish, her words tumbling over each other. "Jean-Pierre... por favor... más."

His reply came in soft whispers, his tone soothing and commanding all at once. "Reste avec moi... laisse-moi te montrer..."

Her nails raked gently down his back as she gasped. "Mon dieu... tu es... mieux que ton frère."

He paused, raising his head to meet her gaze with a faint smirk. "That again? Should I take it as a compliment?"

She laughed, pulling him back to her. "Take it however you want, just don't stop. "Metemelo, metemelo Amor"."

Her voice softened as the intensity between them grew. "Jean-Pierre... Je suis à toi."

"Et tu es à moi," he whispered in return, his voice steady as they moved together in rhythm.

THE AFTERMATH

They lay tangled in the sheets, the room silent except for the sound of their slowing breaths. Her head rested against his chest, her fingers tracing circles on his skin.

"Jean-Pierre," she said softly, her voice carrying a smile, "you don't disappoint."

"Neither do you," he replied, brushing a strand of hair from her face.

She tilted her head to look at him, her expression half-teasing, half-serious. "You know this doesn't solve anything, right?"

He sighed, his hand stilling on her back. "No, but it doesn't make it worse either."

Her lips curved slightly, and she shifted closer. "Tomorrow, we'll deal with the mess. Tonight..."

"Tonight, let's not think about it," he finished for her.

She nodded, resting against him once more. As exhaustion crept in, Jean-Pierre let his eyes close, the weight of the world momentarily lifted.

07 TRAVEL TO THE FINCA

B y morning, they lay tangled in the sheets, the early light streaming through the curtains. Sandra's finger traced idle patterns on Jean-Pierre's chest as she stared into his eyes.

"Can you help me get to the USA?" she asked softly.

Jean-Pierre blinked, her question catching him off guard. "The USA?"

"Yes," she said, her voice a mix of hope and caution. "If I take you to Muskcobar, will you help me get there?"

Jean-Pierre sighed, rubbing his temple. "It's not that simple, Sandra. You'll need a visa, and even with connections, it's a long—"

She cut him off with a sly smile. "I've heard about a man whose wife, Melania, got into the U.S. without any trouble. Maybe you could ask him?"

Jean-Pierre frowned. "Who are you talking about?"

"Never mind," she said quickly, dismissing the subject with a wave of her hand. "His name's Donald, a friend of mine. Yes, I can ask him but what matters is Muskcobar. Can you really help me?"

Jean-Pierre sat up, the weight of her request pressing down on him. "Can you actually take me to Muskcobar?"

Sandra nodded firmly. "Let me make a few calls. Meet me at lunchtime. And one more thing..."

"What's that?"

"Pack your suitcase—and hide the cocaine inside. We're going to Medellín."

Jean-Pierre's heart skipped a beat. The name alone sent a shiver down his spine. "Medellín," he murmured.

Sandra smirked as she began dressing, her movements deliberate and confident. "Don't look so worried, gringo. Muskcobar likes his guests. Most of the time."

ARRIVAL IN MEDELLÍN

Sandra and Jean-Pierre stepped off the plane into the humid air of Medellín. The bustling Río Negro Airport buzzed with activity, but Jean-Pierre couldn't shake the unease that had been building since they boarded the flight.

At the rental car counter, Sandra took charge, securing a sleek SUV for their journey.

"Where are we going?" Jean-Pierre asked as she slid into the passenger seat.

Sandra shot him a cryptic smile. "Maybe to paradise. Maybe to hell. Isn't life exciting?"

Jean-Pierre chuckled nervously, gripping the wheel as they navigated the winding roads toward Guatapé.

They arrived at a quaint hotel near the iconic Piedra del Peñol, the towering granite landmark casting long shadows over the lush landscape. A man in a wide-brimmed sombrero approached them in the parking lot.

"This is Juan Carlos," Sandra said, her voice light. "He's taking us the rest of the way."

Jean-Pierre's brow furrowed. "What do you mean 'the rest of the way'?"

Juan Carlos gestured toward a helicopter waiting nearby. "Hop in. We've got a long ride ahead."

They all moved into the helicopter. Two scary looking guys were already inside the helicopter.

The helicopter lifted smoothly into the air, the sprawling Guatapé Reservoir below glinting in the sunlight like a sapphire. Sandra pointed out various landmarks, her voice animated as she explained the history of the area.

"What's that?" Jean-Pierre asked, leaning closer to the window as they passed over a cluster of crumbling structures.

"Pablo Escobar's old La Manuela" Sandra replied. "A ruin now. Some say there's still gold and a few bodies buried there, but no one's brave enough to look, It is government property."

Jean-Pierre nodded, the sight filling him with a mix of fascination and dread.

Before he could comment further, he felt hands grab him roughly from behind. A black hood was yanked over his head, plunging him into darkness.

"Sorry, gringo," a gruff voice muttered. "The rest of the trip is a secret."

Jean-Pierre struggled briefly but stopped when a firm grip held him in place. The rhythmic thrum of the helicopter blades drowned out any other sounds as fear tightened in his chest.

AT THE FINCA

Jean-Pierre was pulled from the helicopter, the hood still in place. The jungle sounds enveloped him: birds calling in the distance, insects humming in the thick air, and the rustle of leaves in the breeze. He stumbled as they guided him toward a vehicle, the humid heat clinging to his skin.

The ride through the jungle was bumpy and disorienting, the earthy smell of wet vegetation filling his senses. He tried to focus, but the uncertainty gnawed at him.

When the hood was finally removed, Jean-Pierre blinked against the light, his vision adjusting. In front of him stood an impressive finca—a sprawling estate surrounded by manicured gardens, armed guards, and luxury vehicles.

"Welcome," a deep voice greeted him.

Jean-Pierre's heart sank as he recognized the man approaching: Muskcobar.

"Hello, gringo," Muskcobar said with a smile that didn't reach his eyes. "I believe you have something that belongs to me."

The bag was opened before Muskcobar. He glanced inside, his smile faltering. "This is it?"

Jean-Pierre swallowed hard. "That's all. The rest... sank."

"Sank?" Muskcobar's laugh was cold and sharp. "That's an interesting way of saying someone stole my share."

Jean-Pierre hesitated, unsure how much to reveal.

"You'll stay here," Muskcobar said, his tone leaving no room for argument. "We'll see how long it takes to find the rest of what's mine."

SETTLING INTO THE FINCA

Jean-Pierre was escorted through the sprawling finca, its opulence starkly contrasting with the tension gripping his chest. The estate was a fortress disguised as a paradise—manicured gardens, a sparkling pool, luxury cars gleaming under the sun, and armed guards positioned strategically at every corner.

"This way, amigo," one of the guards said, nudging Jean-Pierre forward.

As they entered the main house, Jean-Pierre couldn't help but marvel at its grandeur. Marble floors reflected the golden chandeliers hanging above, and the air was perfumed with the faint scent of orchids.

Muskcobar led him to a large dining hall, where Sandra was already seated, her posture relaxed as though she were an honored guest rather than an accomplice.

"Sit," Muskcobar ordered, gesturing to a chair.

Jean-Pierre obeyed; his movements stiff.

"Let's talk business," Muskcobar began, his tone casual but his eyes sharp. "You owe me, gringo. And you're not leaving until I have what's mine."

Jean-Pierre met his gaze, forcing himself to remain calm. "I'll do my best to help you recover what's missing."

Muskcobar leaned back, his lips curling into a sardonic smile. "You'll do more than your best. You'll work for it."

Sandra chimed in, her voice light. "Jean-Pierre is a world-class chef. Maybe you should put him to work in the kitchen."

Muskcobar raised an eyebrow. "A chef?"

Jean-Pierre nodded reluctantly. "Cooking is what I do best."

Muskcobar's grin widened. "He is also the ex-president of the USA" said Sandra and she provided a file to him. "A chef and an ex-president. You're full of surprises, my friend."

The finca's kitchen was a chef's dream—state-of-the-art equipment, endless rows of spices, and fresh ingredients sourced from the finca's gardens. Muskcobar's staff watched curiously as Jean-Pierre took control, his movements confident and precise.

"What's on the menu, Mr. Ex President?" he asked, leaning against the doorframe.

"Coq au vin," Jean-Pierre replied without looking up. "A French classic."

Muskcobar chuckled. "Let's see if it's as good as all I read about you"."

The aroma of garlic, wine, and herbs soon filled the kitchen, drawing Muskobar, The narco boss and his entourage to the dining table. When Jean-Pierre finally served the dish, the room fell silent as the first bites were taken.

"This is... incredible," Muskcobar declared, his voice filled with genuine admiration. "You're not just a chef—you're an artist."

Jean-Pierre allowed himself a small smile. "I'm glad you approve."

Over the next few weeks, Jean-Pierre's culinary talents worked their magic on Pedro and his family. Dinners became events, with the narco king eagerly awaiting each new dish.

Down at the customs office in Bogota, Officer Jorge was tracing the whereabouts of Jean Pierre and his cocaine package. His eyes, along with his team's, were glued to the screen as they followed the precious cargo from Bogota to Medellin and then to the Uraba region.

A few days passed, and the officers were surprised by the sudden shift.

"The coke is moving... it's going back to Medellin?" one officer muttered, frowning at the screen.

The following day, the GPS indicated Bogota.

"Focus on the GPS location," Jorge ordered. "It seems close to us."

Suddenly, the phone rang. Jorge answered, keeping his eyes on the screen.

"Hola, soy Pedro Muskcobar. I want to talk to Jorge."

Jorge stiffened. "Muskcobar? Are you sure?"

"Hola Jorge, thanks for your present, but I do not need it."

Jorge's brow furrowed. "What present?"

"The GPS you put on Jean Pierre's package. Nobody tampers with my goods."

Jorge's hand tightened around the receiver. "Mr. Muskcobar, we will find you. Our military is closing in on your finca. You know we have drones."

A soft chuckle echoed on the line. "Do you? Congratulations, you are winning the drug war, it seems. But look out your window."

Jorge turned to the surveillance screen showing the rooftop cameras. His stomach dropped. A drone hovered silently outside the window, its red-light blinking.

The explosion ripped through the office before Jorge could say a word. Smoke filled the room as alarms blared, but the damage was done. The screen flickered and died.

In his finca, Muskcobar handed the phone back to his lieutenant, shaking his head. "How impolite. It seems he hung up," Muskcobar said, bursting into laughter. "Fucking amateurs."

One evening, Muskcobar leaned back in his chair, patting his stomach. "My friend, you have a gift. Forget New York. Stay here. We'll open restaurants across Colombia. You'll be rich beyond your wildest dreams."

Jean-Pierre's smile faltered. "I appreciate the offer, but I'm not sure I'm ready for that kind of commitment."

Muskcobar's grin faded, his tone turning serious. "Rich, or dead, gringo. The choice is yours. Betray me, and you'll see the latter."

Jean-Pierre nodded; his throat tight. "I understand."

MUSKCOBAR'S OFFER

One evening, after an extravagant meal, Muskcobar called Jean-Pierre into his study. The room was dimly lit, with bookshelves lining the walls and a large mahogany desk dominating the space.

"My friend," Pedro began, his tone measured, "You are not just a chef. You are a man of influence. An ex-president."

Jean-Pierre tensed. "That was a lifetime ago."

"Perhaps," Muskcobar said, swirling a glass of rum in his hand. "But I've always dreamed of something bigger. I want to be the president of Colombia."

Jean-Pierre's brow furrowed. "President? Muskcobar, with all due respect, politics isn't as simple as cooking a meal."

Muskcobar chuckled. "And yet, you managed to lead a country. Surely you can help me."

"I don't think it works that way."

Muskcobar leaned forward, his eyes narrowing. "Help me, amigo, train me, guide me, and I will let you go free. refuse, and you will never leave this finca alive."

Jean-Pierre swallowed hard, the weight of the ultimatum pressing down on him. "I am a chef, not a politician. But... I will do what I can."

Muskcobar grinned, extending a hand. "Good. You'll start tomorrow."

Reluctantly, Jean-Pierre shook his hand.

LIFE AT THE FINCA

Days turned into weeks, and Jean-Pierre's role at the finca solidified. By day, he was Muskcobar's personal chef, crafting elaborate meals that brought a taste of France to the Colombian jungle. By night, he found himself reluctantly giving Muskcobar lessons on public speaking and diplomacy.

"You need to connect with the people," Jean-Pierre explained one evening as they sat on the finca's expansive terrace. The air was warm, the jungle alive with the hum of insects and the distant calls of birds.

Muskcobar frowned, swirling his glass of aguardiente. "Connect? I give them money and jobs. Isn't that enough?"

Jean-Pierre shook his head. "It's not just about what you give. It is about how you make them feel. They need to trust you, believe in your vision."

Muskcobar's eyes narrowed thoughtfully. "And how do I do that?"

"Listen to them," Jean-Pierre said simply. "Understand their needs. Speak to their hearts, not just their pockets."

Muskcobar leaned back, a grin spreading across his face. "You're not just a chef, gringo. You're a philosopher."

Jean-Pierre managed a tight smile, though his stomach churned. Each piece of advice he gave felt like a betrayal of his own values, but refusing Muskcobar was not an option.

COOKING AND CONNECTIONS

The kitchen was Jean-Pierre's refuge, a place to escape the surrounding danger. Muskcobar's family loved his cooking, especially the children who peered into the kitchen with curiosity.

"Chef Jean-Pierre," asked Carolina, Muskcobar's

youngest daughter one afternoon, "are you making meringues today?"

Jean-Pierre smiled. "Only if you promise to behave at dinner."

The little girl giggled and nodded vigorously. "I promise!"

The meals he prepared became events, drawing Muskcobar's closest associates to the table. Conversations were lively, filled with laughter and the clinking of glasses.

For a few hours each day, the atmosphere in the

finca appeared to relax.

"Your coq au vin is better than anything I've ever tasted," Muskcobar declared one evening, his voice booming with approval. "And that clafoutis with cherries? Magnifique!"

Jean-Pierre offered a polite nod, though the praise felt hollow. He wasn't cooking for joy anymore; he was cooking for survival.

One evening, after an extravagant feast, Muskcobar called Jean-Pierre into his private study. The room was dimly lit, the scent of cigar smoke heavy in the air.

"My friend," Muskcobar began, gesturing for Jean-Pierre to sit. "You've proven yourself invaluable. Not just as a chef, but as a thinker, a strategist."

Jean-Pierre raised an eyebrow. "I'm just a man trying to stay alive."

Muskcobar chuckled, pouring two glasses of rum. "And you're doing an excellent job. But I've been thinking... we could do great things together."

"Great things?" Jean-Pierre echoed cautiously.

"Yes." Muskcobar leaned forward, his eyes gleaming with ambition. "Restaurants all over Colombia. A culinary empire. And when I become president, you'll be by my side, guiding me."

Jean-Pierre's chest tightened. "Muskcobar, I'm a chef, not a politician."

"You're both," Muskcobar countered. "And I trust you. But let me be clear—betray me, and there will be no second chances."

Jean-Pierre forced himself to meet Muskcobar's gaze, his voice steady. "I understand."

08 | PRESIDENTIAL ADVISER

PICTURES OF POWER

One humid evening, months into Jean-Pierre's captivity at the finca, Muskcobar summoned him to the grand study. The room was a portrait of excess: dark mahogany shelves crammed with leather-bound books, an antique globe bar stocked with top-shelf liquor, and a crystal chandelier casting a golden glow. The air reeked of leather and cigar smoke, a heavy scent that lingered like an unwelcome guest.

But it wasn't the books or the opulence that caught Jean-Pierre's attention, it was the wall of photographs.

Dozens of frames lined the far wall, showcasing Muskcobar's life among the elite of Colombia's underworld. There he was, shaking hands with a cartel boss whose name Jean-Pierre recognized from infamous headlines. Another photo captured Muskcobar, younger but just as commanding, seated at a table piled with cash and surrounded by armed guards.

"Admiring my gallery?" Muskcobar asked, his voice cutting through the heavy silence.

Jean-Pierre turned; his unease evident. "They're... impressive. But why keep them on display?"

"Why hide history?" Muskcobar replied with a smirk, gesturing for Jean-Pierre to sit. "These men shaped Colombia. Some for better, some for worse. But most of them played the game—and some survived. Like me."

Jean-Pierre remained silent, his gaze drifting back to the photos.

The weight of the room's history was almost palpable, a constant reminder of the stakes.

A Dangerous Proposition

Muskcobar sat behind his massive oak desk, a glass of Aguardiente in one hand and a smoldering cigar in the other. He exhaled a slow plume of smoke before speaking.

"Jean-Pierre," Muskcobar began, his tone smooth and deliberate, "you've turned my finca into a paradise. But you are far more than a chef."

Jean-Pierre shifted uncomfortably in his seat, his crisp chef's coat feeling oddly out of place in the study's intimidating grandeur. "I'm not sure what you mean."

Muskcobar leaned forward, placing the cigar in a crystal ashtray. "A man who became president of the United States without a shred of political experience. Remarkable. Your story is... inspiring."

Jean-Pierre's shoulders tensed. "That was years ago. I'm not that man anymore."

"Maybe not," Muskcobar said with a faint smile. "But the knowledge is still there. The experience. And I intend to use it, elections are next month"

"Make me the best president of South America," Muskobar declared, his voice brimming with conviction.

Jean-Pierre blinked, stunned into silence. "The best President? Muskcobar, I know kitchens, not politics. I can only try."

"You underestimate yourself," Muskcobar said, lighting his cigar again. "You've walked the halls of power, negotiated with titans, and made impossible things happen. I need someone with your understanding of how the game is played."

Jean-Pierre hesitated, the enormity of the proposition sinking in. "Even if I help, politics is... messy. Complicated."

Muskcobar chuckled, leaning back in his chair. "Jean-Pierre, I thrive in chaos. Colombia is ready for a leader who isn't afraid to rewrite the rules." we were promised Peace we ended up in chaos".

The silence between them was heavy, the weight of Muskcobar's ambition settling over the room. Finally, Jean-Pierre spoke, his voice steady. "I'll help you, but on one condition. It has to be limited in time"

Pedro's grin faltered. "And that is?"

"One year and one day," Jean-Pierre said firmly.

The tension was thick as Muskcobar stared at him, unblinking. Then, with a booming laugh, he rose from his chair and extended a hand. "Agreed. One year and one day."

Jean-Pierre shook his hand, the gesture sealing a pact that would change both their lives forever.

THE NARCO SUMMIT

Before launching his campaign, Muskcobar sought support from the narco community. He hosted a gathering at his finca, a spectacle of opulence that showcased his charisma and power.

The women arrived first, dressed in designer gowns from Balenciaga and Dolce & Gabbana. Their jewelry sparkled under the chandelier's glow, and luxury handbags from Dior and Chanel dangled from their arms. Plastic surgery has sculped their natural beauty with added volumes.

The men, no less extravagant, combined rugged charm with ostentation. Cowboy boots with intricate designs clicked against the marble floors, and some carried revolvers adorned with gold and platinum hanging on the side of their large bellies.

Muskcobar greeted them all with the warmth of a gracious host, his charm disarming even the most skeptical "Hola Carlos! Hola Sergio un placer, Hola Gustavo Feliz de verte, Carmen que hermosa, Maryuli espectacular tu vestido…

Jean-Pierre took center stage at the banquet, unveiling his bold concept of "Narco Cuisine."

"I present to you," Jean-Pierre began, gesturing to the spread before him, "the future of Colombian gastronomy."

First came "The Muskcobar Cocktail", a daring blend of Aguardiente, passion fruit, and a hint of cocaine. Its vibrant orange hue caught the light, and Muskcobar raised his glass in approval.

Next was the Marijuana-Infused Salad, an artistic medley of greens drizzled with cannabis-infused olive oil. Its boldness drew gasps and nods of approval.

Jean-Pierre continued with Mantequilla Marijuana, a rich butter infused with marijuana, served on warm, freshly baked bread.

The room buzzed with admiration, and Muskcobar couldn't hide his pride.

"A toast!" he declared. "To innovation!"

Jean-Pierre raised his glass, his voice calm but commanding. "To a future where food and power come together."

Muskcobar clapped him on the back, grinning. "You, my friend, are the Michelangelo of the kitchen. You have turned controversy into art."

Jean-Pierre smirked. "And you, Muskcobar, are the Michelangelo of cocaine. I am just keeping up."

The room erupted in laughter, and Muskcobar leaned closer, his tone soft but firm. "Together, we'll change everything."

A VISION FOR COLOMBIA

The strategy session began immediately, the room buzzing with Muskcobar' s palpable energy. He paced in front of the oak desk, gesturing broadly as he outlined his plan. His voice, a mix of charisma and conviction, carried the weight of a man determined to rewrite history.

"Jean-Pierre," Muskcobar began, stopping to jab a finger at the air, "Do you realize what we're sitting on? Colombia's cocaine industry generates $18.2 billion every year—as much as our oil exports. And what are we doing with it? Wasting it. Bribes, seizures, burned goods... everyone loses."

Jean-Pierre leaned forward; his brow furrowed. "And you think taxing it will fix that?"

"Not think," Muskcobar corrected, his voice rising with passion. "I know. A 10% tax would bring in $1.8 billion annually. That's more than enough to build hospitals, fund schools, repair roads—we could transform Colombia into a modern nation."

Jean-Pierre folded his arms, skeptical. "And what about the people who are profiting from it now? The cartels? The military? They won't just roll over and let you take their piece of the pie."

Muskcobar stopped pacing, his face hardening as he met Jean-Pierre's gaze. "The military already profits from this game. They will see reason when they understand that my plan ensures their survival and expands their influence. As for the cartels..." He smirked, his confidence chilling. "Let's just say I've survived worse than a few disgruntled traffickers."

Jean-Pierre did not look convinced. "You are talking about dismantling decades of corruption and violence. That is not just a policy change—it's an upheaval."

"Exactly," Muskcobar replied, his voice unwavering. "And that is why it will work. People are tired of the status quo. They are tired of broken promises, tired of seeing their loved ones die for a drug war that benefits no one but the corrupt."

Jean-Pierre pressed his fingers to his temple, trying to piece together the enormity of Muskcobar's vision. "Even if you convince the power players, how do you sell this to the average citizen? Legalized cocaine will not be an easy pitch."

Muskcobar' s grin widened, his tone taking on an almost playful edge. "By taxing everything. Extortion, kidnapping, prostitution, human trafficking—every illegal activity that lines the pockets of criminals. We turn them into revenue streams for healthcare, education, and infrastructure. This is not just a campaign—it's a revolution for the people. A campaign to take back what's been stolen from them." I am working on a franchise of brothels contributing 10% of their income to mothers in need.

Jean-Pierre raised an eyebrow. "So, you're proposing to tax the crimes that have torn this country apart and call it progress?"

"No," Muskcobar replied, his voice firm. "I'm proposing to control them. Regulate them. End the chaos. What is better: a black market that thrives in the shadows, or a system that benefits the nation? The people will see the difference when their children have schools, when their streets have lights, when their hospitals can actually save lives of the average citizen and spend less resources on gun fight victims."

"I heard you wanted to tax selfies and impose a permit to have children when you were president of America, I follow your footsteps"

Jean-Pierre leaned back in his chair, his thoughts swirling. Muskcobar' s vision was undeniably bold, even revolutionary. But the risks were staggering, the enemies formidable. "You'll make enemies," he said quietly.

Muskcobar let out a dry chuckle, his smile tinged with grim determination. "I've already made them," he said. "But this is not about power, Jean-Pierre. It is about legacy. I want to be the Bolívar of our time, the man who transformed Colombia for good."

"The Bukele of South America"? suggested Jean Pierre.

"Much more than that"

Jean-Pierre sat in silence for a long moment, studying the man before him. Muskcobar' s passion was undeniable, but so was the danger that came with it. "And what happens if it fails?" he asked finally.

"It won't," Muskcobar replied, his tone leaving no room for doubt. "Because failure isn't an option when the future of a nation is at stake."

For the first time, Jean-Pierre allowed himself to wonder: Could this actually work? Could this man, for all his faults, truly bring the change Colombia so desperately needed? The answers were not clear, but one thing was certain—he had just become part of something far bigger than he had ever imagined.

CAMPAIGN AND VICTORY

The campaign swept through Colombia like a tidal wave. Muskcobar' s slogan, "Make Antioquia Great Again", wasn't just a tagline—it was a rallying cry that resonated across the nation. Town squares filled to the brim with hopeful faces, many holding makeshift signs scrawled with his name. In rural villages, where roads were mere dirt paths and electricity was sporadic, Muskcobar' s team distributed fliers promising schools, clean water, and paved roads. In bustling cities, his rallies became spectacles, complete with music, banners, and Muskcobar himself commanding the stage with the ease of a seasoned performer.

"Colombia has been bled dry for decades," Muskcobar declared at a rally in Medellín, his voice echoing across the packed plaza. "We have suffered under corruption, crime, and broken promises. No more! It's time to reclaim our future!"

The crowd roared, their chants of "Muskcobar! Muskcobar!" reverberating like thunder. His charisma was magnetic, his promises bold enough to ignite hope in a population weary of despair.

THE STRATEGIST BEHIND THE SCENES

While Muskcobar captivated the masses, Jean-Pierre toiled in the shadows, crafting policy points and tempering Muskcobar's fiery rhetoric with practical solutions. Late nights were dedicated to reviewing documents, with their discussions frequently marked by intense debates.

"Muskcobar," Jean-Pierre said during one such session, sliding a draft speech across the table. "If you push too hard on the tax reforms, you'll alienate the urban voters."

Muskcobar skimmed the paper, shaking his head. "No, Jean-Pierre. They need to hear the truth, not a watered-down version of it. We are not here to play it safe."

"And we're not here to scare them off," Jean-Pierre countered, his tone firm.

"You can promise change without making them feel like targets. Balance is key."

Muskcobar sighed but relented, nodding. "Fine. Rewrite it. But keep the heart of it intact. This is a revolution, not a compromise".

"Will you buy votes, asked Jean Pierre?"

"No, we will distribute vouchers we pay only if we win" he smiled.

Their partnership, though unlikely, was undeniably effective. Jean-Pierre brought discipline and strategy to Muskcobar' s boundless energy, while Muskcobar' s charisma gave Jean-Pierre's careful planning the force it needed to resonate with the public.

ELECTION NIGHT

When the results were announced, Colombia erupted. In Bogotá, fireworks painted the night sky as crowds filled the streets, waving flags and singing. In Antioquia, people danced in the plazas, their joy spilling over like the Aguardiente bottles being passed around.

At the heart of it all stood Muskcobar, now President Muskcobar, on the grand balcony of the Capitolio Nacional. The light from a thousand phones and cameras illuminated his triumphant figure as he raised his hands, commanding the jubilant crowd below.

"Today," he began, his voice booming through the loudspeakers, "we begin a new chapter for Colombia. A chapter of hope, of progress, and of unity. Together, we will build a nation that honors its people and reclaims its destiny!"

The crowd roared their approval, their chants growing louder with every word. Muskcobar paused, letting the cheers wash over him, a faint smile tugging at the corners of his mouth.

A QUIET REFLECTION

Several weeks went by in the kitchen of the finca, as Jean-Pierre observed the broadcast on a large television screen. The roar of the crowd filtered faintly through the window, mixing with the scent of coq au vin simmering on the stove.

Sandra appeared in the doorway, a glass of wine in her hand. "We are missing the Post election celebrations," she said, leaning casually against the frame.

Jean-Pierre turned with a contemplative expression. "Muskcobar does not require my assistance for that part. My task is complete."

Sandra stepped inside, setting her glass down on the counter. "You helped him win; you know. Without you, he would still be shouting slogans in some dusty town square."

Jean-Pierre smiled faintly, turning back to the stove. "Maybe. But the hard part is just beginning."

She tilted her head, studying him. "You do not seem thrilled. Regrets already?"

He stirred the pot, his movements deliberate. "No regrets. Just... uncertainty. Muskcobar dreams big, but reality does not always cooperate."

Sandra placed a hand on his shoulder, her touch light but grounding. "You have been through worse.

And besides, you have cooked your way into history. That has got to count for something."

Jean-Pierre chuckled softly, plating the dish with precision. "History tastes better with butter."

Sandra laughed, her voice a bright counterpoint to the distant roar of the crowd. For a moment, in the warmth of the kitchen, Jean-Pierre allowed himself a quiet sense of accomplishment. Outside, the nation celebrated the beginning of a new era, one that he had helped shape—however reluctantly.

CONFLICTED LOYALTIES

In the quiet moments after dinner, Sandra often found Jean-Pierre in the kitchen, her presence a mix of comfort and complication.

"You're doing well," she said one night, leaning against the counter as he cleaned up.

"Well, enough to survive," Jean-Pierre replied, his tone heavy.

Sandra's expression softened as she stepped closer. "You have impressed him, you know. Muskcobar does not trust easily, but he trusts you."

Jean-Pierre glanced at her, his hands stilling. "And you? Do you trust me?"

She smiled faintly, reaching out to touch his arm. "I trust you more than I've trusted anyone in a long time."

Their connection deepened in the stolen hours of the night, their whispered conversations and shared silences offering a brief reprieve from the chaos of their lives.

"You're a French artist," Sandra murmured one evening, her head resting on his chest. "In the kitchen and in... other places."

Jean-Pierre chuckled softly, pressing a kiss to her hair. "And you, my treasure, are a Latin masterpiece."

Despite their moments of intimacy, Jean-Pierre couldn't shake the weight of his predicament. Muskcobar' s threats loomed over him, a constant reminder that his freedom and his life hung by a thread.

09 | TROUBLE IN THE ISLAND

SYLVIE'S LIFE WITH LARRY

Sylvie's life with Larry had seemed idyllic in the beginning. Together, they had purchased the "Privilege II" a sleek and modern catamaran, and launched a business chartering trips between St. Martin and St. Barth. The promise of freedom on the open seas, the allure of exotic islands, and the intimacy of shared adventure felt like a dream.

But the reality of life with Larry was far from what Sylvie had imagined.

Once the charming and spontaneous adventurer, Larry had become a domineering macho, treating Sylvie more like a subordinate than a partner. He barked orders with the authority of a captain commanding a crew, while Sylvie spent her days scrubbing the deck, climbing the mast to untangle sails, and fixing equipment. Larry, meanwhile, indulged in rum and marijuana, swapping boating tales with friends while neglecting her entirely.

"You love the sea, don't you?" Larry had said once, laughing as he sprawled out on the deck. "Well, it loves you too—because it makes you work harder than anyone else, I know!"

Sylvie's frustration grew, her dreams of a romantic, adventurous life slipping further out of reach. Trapped financially and emotionally, she clung to the hope that things would improve.

THE STORM APPROACHES

It was late afternoon when Sylvie noticed the wind picking up. Dark clouds loomed on the horizon, the waves swelling ominously.

She was on deck, struggling to secure the awning when Larry stumbled aboard, tipsy as usual.

"What the hell are you doing?" Larry barked; his voice slurred. "We're not going anywhere."

Sylvie glared at him, her grip tightening on the ties. "There is a storm coming, Larry. A hurricane."

"Hurricane?" Larry squinted at the horizon, the waves crashing louder against the hull of "The Privilege II". "Don't trust the damn weather reports. They do not know what they're talking about."

"This one's real," Sylvie shot back. "It is called Hurricane. "Hurricane Emmanuel". Category five."

Larry dismissed her with a wave. Our "Privilege II" can manage it. Now make me a sandwich. I am starving."

Sylvie bit back her anger, retreating to the galley to prepare something. But as she returned with a plate of sandwiches, the boat rocked violently, the wind screaming through the rigging.

"It's getting worse," she said, her voice shaking.

"Shut up, Sylvie!" Larry snapped; his eyes glued to the computer screen displaying weather updates. "Maybe if I'm lucky, Hurricane Emmanuel will blow you back to New York."

Sylvie's eyes burned with tears, but she refused to let them fall.

DISASTER STRIKES

As evening fell, Hurricane Emmanuel roared to life with unrelenting fury. The "Privilege II" was no match for the storm's rage, bucking and groaning as the waves crashed against its hull. The wind howled like a relentless predator, shaking the catamaran to its core. The tangled sail on the main mast whipped violently, a loud crack echoing every time the wind caught its frayed edges.

Larry stood on deck, beer in hand, squinting at the chaos around him. His face was red, either from alcohol or sheer determination replacing common sense.

"I have to climb up and fix that damn sail," he muttered, more to himself than to Sylvie.

Sylvie, gripping the edge of the boat for balance, looked at him in disbelief. "Larry, are you out of your mind? It is too dangerous!"

He turned to her sharply, his voice rising above the storm. "Do as I say! Start the engines and lift the anchor!"

Fear gripped her, but she obeyed, her hands trembling as she worked. The rain lashed at her face, soaking her clothes as she fumbled with the controls. The engine sputtered to life, its low hum barely audible over the deafening storm.

Larry, meanwhile, strapped himself into his harness, muttering curses under his breath. "Keep the bow into the wind!" he shouted; his words carried away as quickly as they left his mouth.

Sylvie glanced up, her stomach twisting in knots as Larry began his perilous climb up the 70-foot mast. The catamaran swayed violently, each gust of wind threatening to toss him into the raging sea below.

"Larry, please! Come down!" she screamed, but he ignored her, his focus fixed on the tangled sail above.

A monstrous wave loomed in the distance, its crest glowing white against the darkened sky. Sylvie's eyes widened in terror.

"Larry!" she shrieked, her voice breaking.

The wave slammed into the «Privilege II» with the force of a freight train. The boat lurched sideways, the mast bowing under the strain. Larry's harness snapped with a sickening pop, and he plummeted toward the deck.

The sound of his body hitting the wood was gut-wrenching a dull, heavy thud that seemed to echo even over the storm.

"My hip!" Larry groaned, writhing in pain as he clutched his side. His face was contorted in agony, his breaths coming in shallow gasps. "I think it's broken. Damn it, Sylvie, help me!"

Sylvie rushed to his side, her heart pounding in her chest. "Larry, oh my God... I'll get you to the dock. Just hold on."

"You have to," he rasped, his voice weak. "I cannot move. Just... get me off this damn boat You stupid frog."

A FIGHT FOR SURVIVAL

The storm showed no mercy. The wind screamed, and rain pelted Sylvie as she took the wheel. Her hands trembled as she fought to steer the catamaran toward the dock.

"Keep the bow into the wind!" Larry yelled; his voice strained with pain.

"I'm trying!" Sylvie shouted back; her knuckles white as she gripped the wheel.

The catamaran pitched violently, each wave threatening to capsize it.

Sylvie's inexperience and the storm's ferocity made navigation nearly impossible. The wheel fought her at every turn, and the boat groaned under the relentless assault of the waves.

As the dock came into view, a sudden gust of wind pushed the "Privilege II" off course. Sylvie gritted her teeth, pulling the wheel with all her strength to correct their path.

"Get it together, are you stupid Sylvie!" Larry barked, his voice cutting through the chaos. "We're almost there!"

But the storm had other plans. Another massive wave slammed into the side of the boat, throwing Sylvie off balance.

The "Privilege II" careened toward the dock, the carbon fiber structure looming closer with terrifying speed.

"Slow down! You are going to crash!" Larry shouted, his face pale with fear.

"I can't!" Sylvie cried, panic flooding her voice.

The hull of "The Privilege II" slammed into the dock with a deafening crunch. Carbon fibers and wood debris splintered, and the boat rocked violently, nearly tipping over. Sylvie was thrown against the wheel, her breath knocked out of her as she hit the controls. Water surged over the deck, flooding the cockpit.

RESCUE AND LOSS

The sound of voices cut through the storm. Sailors onshore had rushed to the dock, braving the elements to help. Ropes were tossed onto "The Privilege II", and hands reached out to steady the battered catamaran.

"Help him!" Sylvie yelled, pointing to Larry, who was slumped against the railing, clutching his side.

With heroic efforts, the sailors managed to lift Larry onto a makeshift stretcher. His groans of pain were nearly drowned out by the storm as they carried him toward the waiting ambulance.

"Be careful!" Sylvie called after them, her voice cracking.

As the ambulance disappeared into the night, Sylvie stood on the dock, soaked and trembling. "The Privilege II" swayed precariously, its hull badly damaged, water pooling in its hold.

The hurricane's fury had not yet abated, and Sylvie could not shake the sinking feeling that the worst was still to come.

THE WRATH OF HURRICANE EMMANUEL

Across the island, "Hurricane Emmanuel" tore through St. Maarten with unrelenting force.

At the children's restaurant in Grand Case, Jacqueline et Patrick were paralyzed with fear, intense winds were blowing forcefully, impacting the walls and causing the windows to break. Water surged into the dining room, sweeping away chairs, tables, and the steel drum band's instruments.

Patrick yelled over the chaos, "Jacqueline, get behind the counter! Now!"

Jacqueline grabbed his arm. "Patrick, the roof—"

Before she could finish, part of the ceiling collapsed with a deafening crash. Patrick shielded her, his heart pounding as debris rained down around them.

As the eye of the hurricane passed, an eerie silence fell over the restaurant. The siblings exchanged a glance, both knowing the worst was yet to come.

When the storm surged again, it was relentless, finishing what it had started.

By dawn, Jacqueline et Patrick was a hollow shell, its vibrant charm reduced to rubble.

RETURN TO RUINS

Ten days after the storm, Sylvie pushed Larry back to the marina. His leg was in a cast. The air was heavy with the scent of salt and destruction.

The once-bustling dock was now a graveyard of broken boats and scattered debris. Mangled masts jutted out of the water like skeletal remains, and the few vessels that survived were battered beyond recognition.

Sylvie stopped abruptly at the slip where The Privilege II had been moored, her stomach twisting in dread.

The boat was gone.

"No," she whispered, her voice trembling. "It can't be..."

Larry craned his neck, his face darkening with rage. "What the hell? Where is the catamaran?"

Sylvie stepped closer, her eyes scanning the water in desperation. The frayed ropes that once tethered "The Privilege II" dangled uselessly.

"Maybe it broke loose," she suggested weakly.

"Broke loose?" Larry barked. "Someone stole it, Sylvie! Everything we had was on that boat!"

Sylvie bit her lip, fighting back tears. The devastation left by Hurricane Emmanuel had already taken so much, and now it seemed even their dreams had been swept away.

A RUINED DREAM

In Grand Case, Patrick and Jacqueline stood amidst the ruins of their restaurant. The sun, ironically bright, revealed the full extent of the hurricane's wrath. Twisted metal, shattered glass, and waterlogged furniture littered the site.

Patrick picked up a piece of debris, his expression grim. "It's gone," he said quietly.

Jacqueline placed a hand on his shoulder, her voice trembling. "We will rebuild, Patrick. Somehow, we will rebuild."

Patrick's jaw tightened, his resolve hardening. "We have to. It's what Papa would expect of us."

10 ORMIGAS CULONAS

EXODUS FROM THE STORM

The morning after Hurricane Emmanuel is a cruel awakening. St. Martin, once a jewel of the Caribbean, now resembles a war zone. Streets lie in ruin, choked with debris. Fallen palm trees scatter like splinters from a shattered puzzle, corrugated roofs crumple into twisted heaps, and shards of glass glint menacingly under the weak sunlight. The once-vibrant hum of island life—the laughter of tourists, the rhythmic beat of calypso music, the chatter from beachside cafés—has vanished. In its place, an eerie silence lingers, broken only by the distant thrum of rescue helicopters and the occasional wail of despair.

Jacqueline steps forward cautiously, her sandals sinking into the thick mud. The dining room, once alive with the clinking of glasses and warm laughter, is unrecognizable. Tables and chairs lie in splintered ruins, tangled in a mess of wood and metal. The floor is a sodden mosaic of broken tiles, drenched menus, and scattered leaves.

Patrick kneels beside the wreckage and picks up a jagged piece of a chair leg, gripping it tightly, as if it might anchor him in the chaos. His shoulders tremble. His voice comes out in a whisper, raw with disbelief.

"It's gone," he murmurs. "Everything we built… it's all gone."

The following hours are spent salvaging what they Could some photos, a cookbook, and dry clothes.

Each rescued item feels like a fragile link to a past that now seems impossibly distant.

When Jean Pierre was informed, he immediately

requested Muskcobar to send one of his planes to rescue them.

By the time the private jet arrives, the sun hangs low on the horizon, painting the sky in hues of orange and pink. A stern-looking pilot in aviator glasses signals for them to board while security holds back desperate onlookers from forcing their way onto the aircraft.

Patrick hesitates at the bottom of the steps, his gaze lingering on the remnants of the Island. His voice is barely audible over the roar of the plane.

"This was supposed to be our future."

Jacqueline takes his hand, squeezing firmly. "Our future isn't tied to this place, Patrick. It's tied to us—to our family. Come on."

The journey to Colombia is anything but smooth. After a brief stop in Curaçao to refuel, they fly into turbulent skies, the storm's lingering wrath making the trip treacherous. Yet as the lush green hills of Colombia finally come into view, a fragile sense of hope begins to take root.

When they landed at a hidden airstrip, Jean-Pierre stands waiting, arms outstretched. The finca behind him, bathed in the soft glow of twilight, is a stark contrast to the destruction they left behind—a sanctuary nestled among rolling hills, its white walls untouched by chaos.

Jean-Pierre pulled them both into a tight embrace, his presence solid and unwavering. "You're safe now," he says. "We'll get through this. Together."

Patrick glanced around, the weight of their loss still pressing on his chest. But when his eyes meet his father's, something shifts. Hope flickered.

Jacqueline took a deep breath, the crisp Colombian air filling her lungs. "This isn't the end," she says firmly. "It's a new beginning."

Jean-Pierre smiles, pride shining in his eyes. "Exactly. And we'll make it better than before."

Standing on the finca's steps, uncertainty still stretching before them, one truth remains—they will face it as a family.

AT MUSKCOBAR'S FINCA

The Jeep climbed a winding path, flanked by coffee plantations and towering palms, until the estate came into view. Muskcobar' s finca was a picture of opulence, its sprawling grounds meticulously manicured. A long driveway lined with lanterns led to the main house, an imposing structure of dark wood and stone.

Patrick let out a low whistle as they stepped out of the car. "Subtle," he muttered sarcastically.

Jacqueline elbowed him, her eyes scanning the grandeur. "Do not start, Patrick. Let us just get through this."

As they neared the entrance, guards opened the

heavy wooden doors. Inside, chandeliers illuminated marble floors, while the air carried scents of fresh flowers and cigar smoke.

Muskcobar greeted them with his usual charm, his white guayabera crisp and immaculate. He spread his arms wide, his smile as practiced as it was disarming.

"Welcome, welcome! Jean-Pierre's children. You've had quite the journey, no?"

Jacqueline managed a polite smile. "Thank you for having us, Senior Muskcobar."

Patrick's gaze flickered to the walls, where a series of photographs caught his attention. Muskcobar was pictured shaking hands with infamous figures—drug lords whose faces had graced countless headlines. One particularly striking photo showed him beside El Chapo, both men grinning over a table laden with cash and weapons.

Patrick couldn't help himself. "Nice décor," he said dryly, nodding toward the photos.

Muskcobar followed his gaze and chuckled, unbothered. "Ah, memories," he said, walking toward the wall. "These men were legends in their time. Flawed, yes, but who among us isn't? History will judge us all, won't it?"

Jacqueline nudged Patrick sharply, her eyes pleading for him to hold his tongue.

"I like your spirit, Patrick," Muskcobar continued, turning back to face them. "You remind me of your father. He was skeptical of me too, at first. But he learned to see the bigger picture."

Patrick raised an eyebrow. "And what picture is that?"

Muskcobar' s smile widened. "The picture of survival. Of taking what life gives you and turning it into gold."

Jacqueline stepped forward; her tone diplomatic. "We have been through a lot, Senior Muskcobar. We are just hoping for a chance to start over."

"And you shall have it," Muskcobar replied smoothly, gesturing for them to follow him deeper into the finca. "But first, let's discuss the terms of that fresh start."

PLATA O PLOMO

Dinner was served on a table that could have belonged in a palace. Crystal glasses sparkled under the warm glow of a chandelier, and silver platters held steaming arepas, roasted meats, and fragrant bowls of salsa. Muskcobar poured wine into the glasses.

Patrick and Jacqueline sat stiffly; their plates untouched. Jean-Pierre, seated between them, seemed to shrink in his chair, his usually controlling presence dulled by the weight of the moment.

Muskcobar swirled his wine glass, studying the siblings with an unsettling smile. "I hear you've had a tough time," he began, his voice almost sympathetic. "The hurricane. The restaurant. A shame, truly."

Patrick bristled at the casual tone, his fingers tightening around the edge of the table. "It's more than a shame," he snapped. "We've lost everything."

Muskcobar's expression did not falter. If anything, his eyes gleamed with amusement. "You haven't lost everything," he said, setting his glass down with deliberate care. "You still owe me."

Jacqueline froze; her fork suspended mid-air. "Owe you?"

Jean-Pierre shifted uncomfortably, his pale face betraying his unease. "Muskcobar, they are just adolescent. They had nothing to do with this."

Muskcobar leaned back in his chair, his smile widening. "But they are your children, Jean-Pierre. And your debt is their debt. That's how family works."

Patrick peevishly, the plates rattling with the impact. "What do you want from us?"

Muskcobar chuckled, unfazed by the outburst. "Relax, hijo," he said smoothly, gesturing for Patrick to sit back down. "I am not a monster. I do not want blood. I want opportunity. And I think I have found the perfect one—for all of us."

Muskcobar paused in front of a particular photo. It showed him proudly holding a tray of steaming dishes, each plate intricately arranged. "This," he said, tapping the glass of the frame with a ringed finger, "is the future."

Jacqueline frowned; her confusion was evident. "What is it?"

"Ortigas culonas," Muskcobar announced, his grin spreading. "Big-bottomed ants. A delicacy in Santander. A dish that could revolutionize Colombian cuisine on a global scale."

Patrick blinked, his brows knitting together. "You're kidding, right?"

"Not at all," Muskcobar replied, turning back to the table. "Imagine a chain of restaurants serving these ants. Protein-packed, environmentally friendly, and exotic enough to intrigue the wealthy and adventurous. We market it as the ultimate Colombian delicacy. Tourists will flock to taste it."

Jacqueline's skepticism was written all over her face. "You want us to run restaurants... serving ants?"

"Not just restaurants," Muskcobar said, his tone growing animated. "An empire. A brand that represents the soul of Colombia. And who better leads it than the Labaguettes? Your family name already carries culinary Privilege. Combine that with my vision, and we will be unstoppable."

Jean-Pierre finally spoke, his voice hoarse. "And if they refuse?"

Muskcobar' s demeanor turned icy, the room growing noticeably tense. "Refusal is not an option, Jean-Pierre. You know that." He leaned forward, his voice dropping to a chilling whisper. "Plata o plomo. Silver or lead. The choice is theirs."

Patrick stood abruptly, his chair scraping loudly against the floor. "You're unfair," he said, his voice low but furious.

Jacqueline grabbed his arm, her grip firm. "Patrick, sit down," she said urgently, her eyes pleading.

Muskcobar watched them both, his smile returning as he straightened his posture. "This isn't a punishment," he said, his tone light once more. "It is a partnership. One that benefits all of us. You get to rebuild, to rise from the ashes of your loss. And I get to create something extraordinary.

Jean-Pierre sighed heavily, rubbing his temples. "You'll fund this... project?"

"Completely," Muskcobar confirmed, spreading his hands. "No loans, no interest. Just loyalty and hard work."

Jacqueline exchanged a look with Patrick. Her voice was soft but resolute. "We will do it. For now."

Muskcobar beamed, clapping his hands together. "Good! I knew you would see reason. Now, let us toast to our future success!"

The siblings raised their glasses with hesitation, as the gravity of their decision loomed over them like a storm cloud.

As Muskcobar grinned and spoke of grand plans, Patrick leaned toward Jacqueline, whispering under his breath. "This isn't over."

Jacqueline nodded subtly; her eyes fixed on their new benefactor. "Not even close," she murmured.

THE DEAL

The morning sun filtered through the thin curtains of their shared room, casting streaks of light across the worn furniture. Patrick paced near the window, his movements restless, his frustration palpable.

"This is ridiculous," he muttered, running a hand through his hair. "He wants us to sell bugs. Bugs, Jacqueline! And if we do not, we're dead."

Jacqueline sat cross-legged on the edge of the bed; her arms wrapped around her knees. "It's not just about us, Patrick," she said, her voice quiet but firm. "If we refuse, Papa pays the price too. You know how Muskcobar operates."

Jean-Pierre sat in a rickety chair in the corner, his hands clasped tightly in his lap. His usually commanding presence was overshadowed by the weight of their predicament. He cleared his throat, drawing their attention.

"Muskcobar' s plan," he began, his voice steady, "is risky, yes. But it is not without merit. Ormigas culonas are not just bugs. They are a delicacy here, a part of Colombian culture. If we approach this the right way, it could work."

Patrick stopped pacing, turning to face his father. His eyes burned with skepticism. "You really believe that, Papa? Can we turn ants into a business?"

Jean-Pierre met his son's intense gaze without flinching. "I believe we do not have a choice. And I believe that if we're going to do this, we have to do it together. We are stronger as a family."

Jacqueline sighed, resting her chin on her knees. "Alright," she said softly. "But if we are going to sell ants, we're going to make them taste like heaven. We will elevate them. Michelin-star quality."

Patrick shook his head, a bitter laugh escaping his lips. "Great. Ants that cost as much as caviar. Sounds like a dream."

Jacqueline raised an eyebrow. "Sarcasm aside, that is the point. We do not just sell ants. We sell an experience something so exclusive, so luxurious, that people will pay top dollar just to say they have tried it."

Jean-Pierre smiled faintly, nodding at his daughter's reasoning. "She is right. If we treat this like a joke, we will fail. But if we approach it with the same passion and precision we put into our restaurant, we can succeed.

Patrick sighed heavily, rubbing the back of his neck. He leaned against the wall, his frustration giving way to reluctant determination. "Fine. Let's do it. But I swear, if Muskcobar suggests bug costumes, I am out."

Jean-Pierre chuckled softly, the tension in the room easing for the first time. "No costumes, Patrick. Just hard work and ingenuity."

Jacqueline smirked, her arms dropping to her sides. "And maybe a few secret recipes. We'll make those ants irresistible."

Patrick rolled his eyes but could not suppress a small smile. "Fine. Deal. But I am not touching any live ones."

Jean-Pierre rose from his chair, his posture regaining some of its old strength. He looked at his children, pride and resolve shining in his eyes. "Then it is settled. We face this challenge head-on. As a family."

They stood together, a united front against the odds stacked against them. The path ahead was uncertain, but for the first time in weeks, hope flickered in the corners of their minds.

THE FIRST STEP

With Muskcobar's backing, the Labaguette family began laying the groundwork for the new venture. Test kitchens were set up in Bogotá, where Jean-Pierre and his children experimented with recipes. They roasted the ants with spices, paired them with gourmet sauces, and even incorporated them into desserts.

Despite the bizarre concept, the results were surprisingly good.

"Who knew ants could taste this good?" Patrick admitted one evening, biting into a crisp, roasted ormiga.

Jacqueline smirked. "Maybe Muskcobar isn't as crazy as he seems."

Jean-Pierre, watching his children work side by side, allowed himself a rare moment of hope. They had lost so much, but perhaps this strange new chapter could be the beginning of something extraordinary.

11 | SYLVIE RETURN

The sun was setting over the sprawling finca, casting long shadows over the manicured lawns and whitewashed walls. Jean-Pierre stood in the kitchen, wiping down the counter after preparing Muskcobar' s evening meal. The sound of cicadas filled the air, blending with the distant hum of the generator.

As he reached for a towel, a movement near the gates caught his eye. A familiar figure was walking up the long dirt path leading to the house accompanied by two body guards. Jean-Pierre squinted, his heart skipping a beat when recognition hit him.

"Sylvie?" he whispered, dropping the towel.

She moved slowly; her steps heavy with exhaustion. Dust clung to her dress, which was torn at the hem, and her once-polished heels were scuffed and muddy. Her hair, usually immaculately styled, hung limply around her face, and her expression was a mixture of desperation and relief.

Jean-Pierre rushed out of the kitchen, his heart pounding as he reached the courtyard. Sylvie stopped as she saw him, her shoulders sagging as if the last of her strength had finally given out.

"Jean-Pierre," she said, her voice cracking.

"Sylvie," he replied, closing the distance between them. He reached out, his hands trembling as they cupped her face. "What happened? Why are you here?"

Tears welled in her eyes, and she shook her head. "I have lost everything, Jean-Pierre. The boat, the money... everything. I had nowhere else to go."

Jean-Pierre pulled her into a tight embrace, his chin resting on her dusty hair. "It's alright," he murmured. "You're safe now."

She clung to him, her body trembling. "I did not know where else to turn. I walked for hours. I just... I could not stop."

Jean-Pierre stepped back, his hands still on her shoulders. "You are here now, and that's what matters. Let us get you cleaned up." May I introduce you to Sandra she is my friend and has helped me so much.

Sylvie looked at her well-dressed manicured and with impeccable make up, she felt unworthy old and exhausted. Sandra took her into her arms "Amiga let me give you some new clothes and freshen up, you are beautiful.

SETTLING IN

Sylvie spent her first night at the finca in the modest guest quarters Jean-Pierre had arranged. The room was clean but sparse, with a single bed, a wooden wardrobe, and a small window that overlooked the vast expanse of Muskcobar's estate. She sat on the edge of the bed, staring at her reflection in the small, cracked mirror on the wall. Her face was drawn, her eyes shadowed by exhaustion and loss.

Jean-Pierre knocked softly before entering, carrying a tray with a simple meal—fresh bread, grilled vegetables, and a glass of water. "You need to eat," he said gently, placing the tray on the small table by the window.

Sylvie gave him a faint smile. "You're still taking care of me after all this time?"

Jean-Pierre shrugged, sitting across from her. "What else is there to do? You have been through enough."

Sylvie reached for the bread, tearing off a small piece. "This place," she said, gesturing vaguely toward the window, "it's a gilded cage, isn't it?"

Jean-Pierre nodded. "It keeps us alive. For now."

She studied him for a moment, her gaze softening. "You have changed, Jean-Pierre. You seem... older. Wiser."

He chuckled, shaking his head. "I've just learned how to survive, and I am in love with Sandra."

THE SEDUCTION

The next morning, Sylvie ventured out into the estate, her steps tentative but purposeful. The finca was an opulent maze of courtyards, fountains, and manicured gardens. Muskcobar was on the terrace, reclining in a sun-drenched chair with a cigar in hand and a glass of rum on the table beside him.

Sylvie approached with deliberate grace, her borrowed dress flowing softly around her, her perfume exhaling seduction. "Good morning," she said, her voice light but confident.

Muskcobar turned, his sharp eyes taking her in. A slow smile spread across his face. "Ah, Sylvie. Jean-Pierre told me you would be staying with us. Welcome."

She sat across from him, folding her hands neatly in her lap. "Thank you, mister President, this estate... it's beautiful."

He gestured broadly, the cigar trailing smoke through the air. "It is a refuge. A place where the

168

noise of the world does not reach, I can relax from my political duties".

Sylvie tilted her head, her smile coy. "And yet you seem like a man who thrives on the action."

Muskcobar chuckled, leaning forward slightly. "Perceptive. I like that. And what about you, Sylvie? What brings you to my little corner of paradise?"

She met his gaze, her expression softening. "I had nowhere else to go. The hurricane took everything. But Jean-Pierre... he has always been my anchor."

"Jean-Pierre is a good man," Muskcobar said, his tone warm but edged with curiosity. "But you... you seem like someone who knows how to navigate storms."

Sylvie leaned closer, her voice dropping slightly. "I have had my share of them. But I have learned that sometimes, it's not enough to weather the storm. Sometimes, you must take control of the ship."

Muskcobar' s grin widened. "I can see why Jean-Pierre speaks so highly of you."

She smiled, her fingers tracing the edge of the table. "And I can see why he's so loyal to you."

Muskcobar poured Sylvie a glass of Aguardiente his movements smooth and deliberate. "Tell me, Sylvie," he said, handing her the glass, "what is it you hope to find here? Surely, you are not just following Jean-Pierre's shadow."

Sylvie took the glass, her fingers brushing his briefly. "I'm not looking for anything," she replied, swirling the amber liquid thoughtfully. "But sometimes, when you stop looking, that's when you find exactly what you need."

Muskcobar' s grin turned wolfish. "And what is it that you need?"

Sylvie raised the glass to her lips, taking a slow sip before meeting his gaze. "A fresh start. A chance to rebuild. And maybe... a reminder that there's still beauty and power in my world."

He chuckled, leaning back in his chair. "You are good. Jean-Pierre said you were clever, but he did not do you justice, you are also very beautiful and sensual."

Sylvie smiled, leaning forward slightly. "Cleverness is not enough. You, Muskcobar, are a man who sees the big picture. That takes vision. Ambition. The kind of ambition that does not just rebuild—it redefines."

Muskcobar' s expression shifted, his interest deepening. "You have a way with words, Sylvie. But ambition... that is a dangerous game, he said as he touched her hand."

"Only if you play it alone," she countered, her voice soft but firm. "But with the right partner? It is unstoppable."

For a moment, Muskcobar studied her, the playful gleam in his eyes giving way to something sharper. "You are not just clever. You are bold."

Sylvie tilted her head, her smile never wavering. "And you are not just powerful. You are exceptional."

THE HOOK

Muskcobar leaned forward, resting his elbows on the table. "You have a unique way of seeing the world, Sylvie. Tell me—what would you do if you had real power?"

Sylvie held his gaze, her lips curving into a small, confident smile. "Power is not about what you have; it's about what you can create. And in this world? The only power worth having is the kind that transforms lives."

Muskcobar raised an eyebrow. "Go on."

"I'd start with the people," she said, her voice steady. "Give them something real. Something they can touch, taste, believe in. You have already built an empire. Imagine if you turned it into a legacy."

He sat back; his expression thoughtful. "A legacy. That's a dangerous word."

"But it's what separates kings from conquerors," Sylvie replied, her tone soft but resolute. "And I think you, Muskcobar, are more than just a conqueror."

Muskcobar' s laugh was low and rich. "Jean-Pierre's not the only strategist in this house, is he?"

Sylvie smirked, finishing her drink. "Sometimes, the best strategy is knowing when to speak... and when to listen."

AMBITION UNLEASHED

Later that evening, Muskcobar summoned Jean-Pierre to his study. The grand room, dimly lit by the warm glow of a single chandelier, smelled of aged rum and expensive cigars. Outside, the finca was quiet, the thick Colombian night settling over the estate like a shroud.

Jean-Pierre entered cautiously, already sensing the weight of the conversation about to unfold. Muskcobar stood by the massive oak desk, swirling a glass of rum, his expression unreadable.

"You called for me," Jean-Pierre said, taking a seat without invitation.

Muskcobar smirked, setting his glass down. "Yes. I have been thinking."

Jean-Pierre exhaled sharply. "That's dangerous."

Muskcobar chuckled, taking a slow sip before continuing. "Winning the presidency was the easy part. Now comes the real work."

Jean-Pierre's eyes narrowed. "You have the power now, Muskcobar. What more do you want?"

The drug lord-turned-president leaned forward; his hands clasped together. "I want to do what no leader before me has had the courage to do. I want to tax everything now."

Jean-Pierre's brow furrowed. "Everything?"

Muskcobar grinned. "Extortion. Prostitution. Drugs Corruption. Even plastic surgery. People are already paying for these things under the table. Why shouldn't the government benefit from it?"

Jean-Pierre leaned back in his chair, running a hand over his face. "You will legalize and tax organized crime?

Muskcobar shrugged. "Colombia is built on the informal economy. The only difference between me and those before me is that I am willing to acknowledge it."

Jean-Pierre sighed. "And the people? Do you really think they will accept this?"

"They'll accept results," Muskcobar said confidently. "New hospitals, better infrastructure, an economy that isn't being drained by hypocrisy." He raised an eyebrow. "They'll call me a revolutionary."

Jean-Pierre hesitated. "And Venezuela? Where does that fit into your 'revolution'?"

Muskcobar chuckled, refilling his glass. "We send beepers to Maduro."

Jean-Pierre blinked. "Beepers?"

"Beepers," Muskcobar repeated, his grin widening. "Just like the Israelis did. We modernize while Maduro and his junta rot in their own incompetence. And then?" He raised his glass. "We take Venezuela. We rebuild Gran Colombia."

Jean-Pierre studied him carefully. "You're talking about war."

Muskcobar shrugged. "I'm talking about destiny."

Jean-Pierre exhaled slowly. "And you want me to make all of this sound... reasonable."

Muskcobar leaned back, his smirk unwavering. "That's why you're here, mon ami. Write me a speech that will make the world believe in the impossible."

A DANGEROUS PROPOSAL

Jean-Pierre remained silent for a long moment, staring at Muskcobar as if searching for some trace of hesitation, some sign that this was mere bravado. But Muskcobar' s gaze was unwavering, his confidence absolute.

"You realize what you're saying?" Jean-Pierre finally spoke, his voice low, careful. "This is not just economic reform. This is rewriting the rules of power. If you go down this road, there is no turning back."

Muskcobar leaned forward, resting his forearms on the desk. "I have never turned back, Jean-Pierre. Not once in my life."

Jean-Pierre drummed his fingers against the chair's armrest, mind racing. "You think you can just waltz into Venezuela, claim it as your own?"

Muskcobar smirked. "Not waltz. Strategize. Control the flow of resources, infiltrate their institutions, turn their own people against them. Maduro's house is already crumbling. We just need to push the last brick."

Jean-Pierre shook his head, more out of disbelief than disagreement. "And you expect me to put this madness into words that won't send the world into panic?"

"I expect you to do what you do best," Muskcobar said smoothly, lifting his glass. "Craft a vision. Inspire. Convince. The same way you made a bunch of criminals believe they deserved a Michelin-star meal, you will make an entire country believe I'm their future."

Jean-Pierre's lips pressed into a thin line. "You know this will put a target on your back."

Muskcobar let out a short, dry laugh. "Jean-Pierre, I was born with a target on my back."

Jean-Pierre inhaled deeply, feeling the weight of what Muskcobar was asking him to do. This was not just about writing a speech. It was about selling an empire, legitimizing a criminal dynasty under the guise of governance. If Muskcobar succeeded, he would not just be the president of Colombia— he'd be the architect of a new world order.

Jean-Pierre leaned forward; his voice quiet but firm. "If I do this, if I give you the words you need, you have to promise me one thing."

Muskcobar raised an eyebrow. "And what's that?"

Jean-Pierre's fingers tightened around the armrest. "That when the time comes, when you've taken everything, you want… you know when to stop."

Muskcobar studied him for a moment before a slow smile spread across his face. "Oh, Jean-Pierre," he said, shaking his head. "You still don't understand, do you?"

He lifted his glass in a silent toast, the flickering candlelight casting deep shadows across his face.

"There is no stopping."

THE WEIGHT OF WORDS

Jean-Pierre sat in the study long after Muskcobar had left, staring at the blank page before him. The candle on the desk flickered, casting shadows along the walls. His mind raced. Muskcobar' s vision was outrageous—insane, even—but it had a strange kind of logic.

A government built on the realities of crime rather than the illusions of law. A leader who wasn't pretending to fight corruption but embracing it as an economic asset. It was madness. But wasn't madness the foundation of every great revolution?

He picked up the pen.

My fellow Colombians, he wrote, for too long, we have lived in denial. We have built a country on hypocrisy, condemning the very industries that sustain us. We cannot erase crime, but we can control it. We cannot eliminate vice, but we can regulate it. We cannot stop the underworld, but we can make it work for us.

The words poured out; each sentence more audacious than the last. He framed Muskcobar' s proposals not as concessions to corruption, but as pragmatic solutions. He turned crime into commerce, vice into industry.

Muskcobar wanted to tax extortion? Jean-Pierre reframed it as "structured security contributions." He wanted to legalize drug trafficking. Jean-Pierre presented it as "nationalized trade regulation." Even taxing plastic surgery was spun into a poetic argument about beauty becoming a national export.

He worked through the night, crafting an argument so compelling that even the most skeptical Colombian would pause to consider it.

By dawn, he had created something terrifyingly persuasive.

THE SPEECH

The next evening, Muskcobar gathered his closest allies in the grand hall of the finca. Smoke curled from cigars, glasses clinked, and the murmur of conversation filled the air. A sense of anticipation pulsed through the room.

Jean-Pierre stood at the head of the long table, his hands resting on the speech. Muskcobar, relaxed and confident, lounged at the other end, sipping his rum.

"This is the speech that will define your presidency," Jean-Pierre said, his voice steady. "Are you sure you're ready for that?"

Muskcobar grinned. "I was born for this."

Jean-Pierre cleared his throat and began to read:

My fellow Colombians, for too long, we have allowed the shadows to dictate our future. Corruption, crime, and poverty have taken root in our soil. But I stand before you today with a vision—a vision of a Colombia that turns its greatest challenges into its greatest strengths.

For decades, our leaders have waged wars they cannot win. They have outlawed what cannot be erased. But the truth is simple: the underground economy is the real economy. And instead of fighting it, we must harness it. We must tax it. We must regulate it. We must make Colombia the first nation to embrace the world as it is—not as we pretend it to be.

We will take the billions hidden in the shadows and bring them into the light. We will fund hospitals, schools, and infrastructure with the very wealth that others would burn. We will not destroy our industries—we will own them.

Silence settled over the room. Even the most skeptical among them looked captivated, as if Muskcobar were already standing before a crowd of thousands.

Then, slowly, Muskcobar began to clap. "Brillant, Jean-Pierre. Absolutely brillant."

From the corner, Sylvie's voice cut through the moment like a blade. "Where did you even learn about all these taxes, Muskcobar? Extortion, prostitution, plastic surgery?" She tilted her head, eyes glinting with amusement. "Sounds suspiciously... French."

Muskcobar let out a booming laugh. "The French know how to monetize everything, don't they, Jean-Pierre?" He smirked, raising his glass. "Maybe I've picked up a thing or two from you.

Jean-Pierre did not respond, only taking a slow sip of his drink.

Muskcobar didn't realize it yet.

But this speech would not just define his presidency.

It would seal his fate.

THE DOWNFALL

In the political opposition, army generals, drug lords. Human traffickers and land owners had planned to get rid of Muskcobar,

A bomb in his car, a rocket on his place, poisoning his food all had been considered the final decision had come a raid on his hide out while he was away from the presidential palace, Cubans mercenaries and Farc soldiers had been hastily recruited and infiltrated the surrounding of the Finca killing Muskcobar guards one by one

The finca sat eerily quiet under the moonless sky, its sprawling estate wrapped in an uneasy calm. Jean-Pierre reclined in Muskcobar' s office, sipping a glass of wine as the drug lord leaned over a map sprawled across the desk.

"Do you think they'll come for me?" Muskcobar asked, his voice growled low.

Jean-Pierre shrugged, setting his glass down. "You are the president, they'll come. The only question is when."

The faint rumble of engines interrupted their conversation. Jean-Pierre froze, his hand hovering over the table. The sound grew louder, unmistakable now—vehicles, heavy ones, storming up the driveway.

Muskcobar's head snapped up. "Madre de Dios," he muttered, reaching for the pistol on his desk.

The first explosion ripped through the finca's gates. Windows shattered, and the air filled with the deafening crackle of gunfire. Jean-Pierre bolted to his feet.

"They're here," Muskcobar said, his voice unnervingly calms despite the chaos erupting around them. "Get your family out. Now."

Jean-Pierre didn't hesitate. He raced through the smoke-filled hallways, shouting, "Sylvie! Sandra!"

He found them huddling near the kitchen, Sandra gripping Sylvie's arm tightly. Both looked up, their faces pale and etched with fear.

"They've come for Muskcobar," Jean-Pierre said, grabbing Sylvie by the shoulders. "We don't have much time. Follow Sandra!"

Sandra nodded; her usual defiance replaced by raw determination. Sylvie clung to her side, shaking.

"Where?" Sylvie demanded.

"The tunnel," Jean-Pierre replied, already leading them toward the hidden passage Muskcobar had shown him months earlier.

The air grew damp and heavy as they descended into the suffocating darkness of the tunnel. At the entrance, Jean-Pierre stopped abruptly.

"What about you?" Sylvie asked, her voice sharp with panic.

Jean-Pierre turned to face her; his eyes soft but resolute. "I'll stay. Muskcobar will need me to be there, and someone has to slow them down."

"Don't be ridiculous!" Sylvie snapped, grabbing his arm. "You'll get yourself killed!"

Jean-Pierre gently pried her hand away, his tone steady. "Sylvie, you and Sandra need to survive. That is what matters now."

Sandra's voice trembled as she spoke. "Jean, please, don't do this."

He cupped her face briefly, a faint smile flickering across his lips. "Take care of yourselves. You will be safe on the other side."

Before either could argue, Jean-Pierre guided them further into the tunnel and sealed the door behind them. As the heavy slab clicked into place, muffling the sounds of chaos above, Sylvie pressed her forehead against the cold stone, tears slipping down her cheeks.

Behind the door, Jean-Pierre stood in the flickering light of the flames, grabbing a Kalashnikov, ready to face whatever came next.

OUTSIDE THE FINCA

Sandra burst into the jungle, pulling Sylvie behind her as branches clawed at their skin. The distant sound of gunfire and explosions thundered through the night like a gathering storm.

"Run!" Sandra hissed her voice sharp with urgency.

Sylvie stumbled over a root, collapsing to her knees with a cry. Sandra spun around and yanked her up, her breath ragged.

"I can't—" Sylvie wheezed, clutching her side.

"You don't have a choice!" Sandra snapped, gripping her arm tightly. "Keep moving!"

The jungle was a tangle of shadows, the faint moonlight barely piercing the canopy. The roar of another explosion lit up the sky behind them, sending a fiery glow flickering through the trees.

Sylvie whimpered, her legs trembling beneath her. "Sandra, I am slowing you down. Leave me!"

"Don't be ridiculous," Sylvie growled, hauling her forward. "We get out of this together. No arguments."

A burst of gunfire cracked in the distance, and Sandra flinched. "Do you think they'll follow us?"

Sandra didn't look back, her grip tightening on Sylvie's arm. "Let's hope they're too busy dealing with Muskcobar."

Another explosion shook the ground beneath their feet, and Sandra forced herself to move faster, dragging Sylvie along. The humid air clung to her skin as her heart pounded in her ears.

"Just a little farther," Sandra murmured, though she had no idea where they were going. "We'll rest when we're safe."

The children stumbled again but pushed herself forward, her face streaked with sweat and tears. Behind them, the finca burned, its glow a beacon of destruction piercing the jungle's darkness.

BACK AT THE FINCA

The firefight had reached its climax. Muskcobar's guards were overwhelmed, their numbers dwindling under the relentless assault. Smoke billowed from the once-pristine courtyard, and the air stank of gunpowder and blood.

Jean-Pierre stood beside Muskcobar as the authorities finally breached the main house. The drug lord, blood streaking from his earlobe, leaned heavily on the desk.

"They've won," Muskcobar said, his voice tinged with bitter amusement.

Jean-Pierre did not reply. He raised his hands as armed officers entered the room, directing their weapons at the two men.

One of them barked an order in Spanish, and Jean-Pierre complied, dropping to his knees. Muskcobar followed suit, wincing as he moved.

As the officers cuffed them, Muskcobar turned to Jean-Pierre with a weary smile. "Well, my friend, it seems the world wasn't ready for me."

Jean-Pierre glanced at him; his face unreadable. "No, Muskcobar. It was not."

They were dragged outside, the finca now a smoldering ruin. As the armored convoy began its journey into the night, Jean-Pierre caught one last glimpse of the estate—the lights fading into the darkness, swallowed by the jungle.

His thoughts drifted to Sylvie and Sandra, running through the forest, and he clung to the fragile hope that they had made it out alive.

12 | JAIL TIME

BEHIND BARS

Jean-Pierre sat on the edge of a narrow bunk, the hard mattress beneath him doing little to ease the ache in his back. The prison cell was dimly lit, its pale-yellow walls stained with years of neglect. A single flickering bulb overhead cast an unsteady light, making the cramped space feel even more suffocating.

Muskcobar leaned lazily against the bars, his grin wide and infuriatingly confident. His impeccably white teeth stood out, a stark contrast to the grime that coated everything else. It was as if Muskcobar's charm remained untouched by the filth surrounding them, a defense mechanism honed over years of survival in places just like this. He knew they would move to a nicer area in a few days.

"Well, Jean-Pierre," Muskcobar drawled, his voice smooth and unbothered, "welcome to our new palace."

Jean-Pierre gestured around the grimy cell, unimpressed. The paint on the walls peeled in long, curling strips, revealing an older, darker layer beneath. The faint smell of sweat, damp concrete, and something metallic hung in the air. "Charming," he said flatly. "A five-star dungeon. You sure know how to pick them."

Muskcobar chuckled, his nonchalant attitude grating against Jean-Pierre's nerves. "Patience, my friend," Muskcobar smirked. "Even the greatest empires start from humble beginnings." He straightened, his hands sliding into his pockets with the air of a man entirely too comfortable in his surroundings.

Jean-Pierre glanced at him; his irritation evident. "Humble beginnings? This isn't some underdog success story, Muskcobar. This is jail. You know, the opposite of success?"

Muskcobar shrugged, unfazed. "Details, details. Every great narrative needs a twist. Call this... Act Two."

"You're insufferable," Jean-Pierre muttered, running a hand through his hair. The strands felt greasy, unwashed after days of confinement, and it only added to his growing frustration.

"And yet," Muskcobar replied with a sly grin, "you're stuck with me."

Jean-Pierre sighed, leaning back against the wall. He studied Muskcobar for a moment, his sharp suit now replaced with the same drab prison uniform they all wore, though somehow, Muskcobar managed to make it look intentional. His charisma, his calm, his maddening refusal to acknowledge the gravity of their situation—it was almost enviable.

"This doesn't bother you at all, does it?" Jean-Pierre asked, his voice low.

Muskcobar tilted his head, a flicker of something unreadable crossing his face. "Bother me? No, mon ami. I've been in worse. This is just... a waiting room."

"A waiting room for what?" Jean-Pierre asked, frowning.

Muskcobar leaned in closer, lowering his voice conspiratorially. "For the next move. The king always plans three steps ahead, my friend. You'd do well to remember that."

Jean-Pierre rolled his eyes, his lips twitching in reluctant amusement. "Just so you know, in chess, the king is one of the weakest pieces."

Muskcobar' s laughter echoed through the small cell, drawing a curious glance from the guard stationed nearby. "Ah, but he is the one piece the game revolves around. Don't forget that Jean-Pierre."

Jean-Pierre closed his eyes for a moment, letting Muskcobar' s words hang in the air. The faint clink of distant cell doors closing and the muffled murmurs of other inmates seeped into the quiet. In the chaos of this place, Muskcobar' s certainty was like an anchor, infuriating yet oddly reassuring.

"You better hope your 'three steps ahead' include getting us out of here," Jean-Pierre finally said, his voice tinged with both sarcasm and resignation.

"Trust me," Muskcobar replied, flashing another one of his maddening grins. "The game's just beginning."

THE WARDEN'S REQUEST

On their third day behind bars, the metallic clatter of keys echoed down the dimly lit hallway. The prison warden—a stocky man with a gleaming mustache that seemed too pristine for his grim surroundings—strode with an air of authority. His hawk-like eyes scanned the cells as he approached, finally stopping outside Jean-Pierre and Muskcobar' s shared space.

"Muskcobar," the warden said, his voice laced with disdain. "I see you're adjusting well to your accommodations."

Muskcobar leaned casually against the wall, his trademark grin firmly in place. "It is cozy. Though the ambiance could use some work. A splash of color, perhaps? Maybe a houseplant?"

The warden ignored the jab, turning his attention to Jean-Pierre. His tone grew sharper. "And you must be the infamous chef Labaguette. A president turned prison guest. Quite a résumé."

Jean-Pierre rose from the bunk, his expression calm but steely. "I was a chef before I was a president, and I'll be a chef long after I leave this place. Is there a point to this visit, or are you just here to savor the irony?"

The warden's mustache twitched slightly, betraying a hint of irritation. "Actually, I need your help. The kitchen staff here are incompetent, and I have heard whispers of your... culinary prowess."

Muskcobar let out a delighted laugh. "Jean-Pierre, the prison's new Michelin-starred chef! Oh, this I must see."

Jean-Pierre sighed, his patience already thinning. "Fine. Show me your so-called kitchen."

The warden led him down a narrow corridor and into a grimy, chaotic room that barely deserved the title of a kitchen. Greasy counters bore the scars of neglect, pots and pans sat in disarray, and a pungent haze of cigarette smoke hung in the air.

Jean-Pierre picked up a rusted ladle, his jaw tightening as he surveyed the scene. "This is what you want me to work with?"

The warden shrugged, unbothered. "It's a prison, not a five-star resort. Do what you can."

Turning to the motley crew of kitchen staff— apathetic inmates who were more interested in their cigarettes than their duties—Jean-Pierre clapped his hands sharply, his voice cutting through the haze. "Alright, listen up! If we are going to do this, we're doing it properly. You—scrub those counters until they shine. You—peel every potato in sight. And someone find me herbs. Anything green that isn't mold."

A wiry inmate leaned against the wall, smirking. "What is this, a spa? You think we are on vacation?"

Jean-Pierre's eyes locked onto the man with a glare so icy it could freeze boiling water. "No, this is a kitchen. And if you do not move now, you'll be the main ingredient in tonight's soup."

The room fell silent, save for the shuffling of feet as the inmates scrambled to follow his orders. Jean-Pierre turned back to the counter, his mind already spinning with ideas to salvage the disaster before him.

Behind him, Muskobar's laughter echoed faintly from the corridor. "That's my guy," he called out, his voice rich with amusement. "Turning a hellhole into haute cuisine!"

LAWYERS BY DAY, ESCORTS BY NIGHT

Late that night, Jean-Pierre and Muskcobar sat in their cell, the air heavy with the faint aroma of roasted chicken that somehow cut through the ever-present scent of despair. On the makeshift table before them sat a tray of chicken, golden and glistening, a miracle Jean-Pierre had conjured from the sorry state of the prison kitchen.

Muskcobar tore into a drumstick with theatrical gusto, rolling his eyes heavenward as if he were dining in a Parisian bistro. "Mon dieu, my friend, you've turned prison cuisine into an art form. Gordon Ramsay would weep."

Jean-Pierre shook his head, a wry smile playing on his lips. "Don't get used to it," he muttered, picking at his own portion. "I am not opening a restaurant here. This was a one-time favor."

Muskcobar leaned back against the wall, licking his fingers with unabashed delight. "Ah, but you could, my friend. Imagine it—Jean-Pierre's Prison Bistro. Reservations required; escape plans optional."

Jean-Pierre let out a low chuckle. "And you'd be the maître d', charming the guests into smuggling us out, no doubt."

Muskcobar' s grin widened, but his tone shifted as he leaned in closer, his voice dropping to a conspiratorial whisper. "Speaking of charming... have you noticed the visitors we get here?"

Jean-Pierre frowned, lowering his chicken. "Visitors?"

Muskcobar raised an eyebrow, his expression almost playful. "Oh, come now. During the day, it's the lawyers, all stiff suits and self-importance. But at night... well, let us just say the shift changes. The escorts arrive." He paused for effect, his grin turning mischievous. "A fascinating rotation, don't you think?"

Jean-Pierre arched an eyebrow, his intrigue piqued despite himself. "Escorts?"

Muskcobar leaned closer with a grin positively devilish now. And he says "I don't know if lawyers are more whore than the prostitutes but they are definitely more expensive and less talented"

Jean-Pierre paused, the corners of his mouth twitching as he fought the urge to laugh. "The lawyers are definitely more expensive... and far less talented."

For a moment, the grim walls of the cell seemed to fade as both men burst into laughter, their shared mirth cutting through the oppressive silence of the prison. The sound echoed down the corridor, drawing curious glances from other inmates.

Muskcobar wiped a tear from the corner of his eye, his laughter subsiding into a satisfied sigh. "Ah, Jean-Pierre, you truly are a man of culture. Even in a place like this, you manage to find humor. That's why we'll survive."

Jean-Pierre shook his head, smirking. "No, Muskcobar, we'll survive because you're too damn stubborn to let us fail. And because I can bribe anyone with good chicken."

Muskcobar raised his drumstick in a mock toast. "To stubbornness and chicken our ticket out of here."

Jean-Pierre clinked his fork against Muskcobar' s makeshift toast, the laughter lingering in the air as they returned to their meal. In the grim confines of their cell, humor was their rebellion, their way of holding on to their humanity because I don't want my preci

MUSKOBAR'S SCHEME

Weeks passed, and Jean-Pierre's culinary skills began to weave an unexpected spell over the prison. The once-hostile dining hall, where tension and aggression ruled, had transformed into a haven of reluctant camaraderie. The aroma of spiced chicken, hearty stews, and fresh-baked bread now filled the air, replacing the metallic stench of despair.

Muskcobar, ever the opportunist, moved through the room like a king in exile, his charisma as magnetic as Jean-Pierre's food was mouthwatering. He laughed with the bullies, shared jokes with the loners, and even managed to soften the wardens with a strategically gifted plate of roast lamb. Alliances formed over every meal, and Jean-Pierre could not help but notice Muskobar's subtle orchestration of it all.

One evening, as the two sat in their usual corner of the bustling cafeteria, Muskcobar leaned in, his voice low enough to escape the ears of prying inmates. "You see it, don't you?" he murmured, gesturing to the room with his fork. "Food is power, Jean-Pierre. You have done more than cook. You have given us leverage."

Jean-Pierre, mid-bite, lowered his fork and gave Muskcobar a long, skeptical look. "Leverage for what?"

Muskcobar' s grin was wolfish, his eyes gleaming with mischief. "Leverage to turn this place into my kingdom."

Jean-Pierre groaned, shaking his head as if he had expected this all along. "I knew it. You are scheming again."

"Always," Muskcobar replied, the corners of his mouth twitching in delight. He raised a chicken leg in a mock toast. "But do not worry, my friend. Every king needs a trusted advisor. And you? You will be the royal chef."

Jean-Pierre chuckled despite himself, leaning back in his chair. "You're impossible."

"And yet, you can't look away," Muskcobar quipped, his grin widening. He took a hearty bite of chicken, his expression that of a man savoring both the taste of victory and the meal itself.

Jean-Pierre sighed, glancing around the dining hall. The laughter, the absence of fights, the strange sense of community—Muskcobar was not entirely wrong. Still, he knew better than to let his guard down.

"Just remember," Jean-Pierre said, pointing a finger at Muskcobar, "when your so-called kingdom crumbles, don't expect me to bail you out."

Muskcobar gave a dramatic bow from his seat, still grinning. "Of course not. I would not dream of it."

But the glint in his eyes told Jean-Pierre otherwise, and he couldn't decide whether to laugh or brace himself for the chaos Muskcobar was undoubtedly about to unleash.

13 | THE ESCAPE

THE PLAN

The walls of the prison buzzed with rumors. Jean-Pierre sat on the edge of his bunk, staring at the cracked ceiling as Muskcobar paced the room like a restless panther.

"They're transferring us tomorrow," Muskcobar said, his voice low and sharp. "Another prison. Less luxury. More restrictions."

Jean-Pierre frowned. "We can't let that happen."

"Exactly," Muskcobar replied, turning to face him. "Which is why we need to act tonight."

Jean-Pierre sighed, leaning forward. "You have a plan, I assume?"

Muskcobar grinned. "Of course. But it involves you doing what you do best."

Jean-Pierre raised an eyebrow. "Cooking?"

"Precisely," Muskcobar said, lowering his voice. "We need something... special. Something that will ensure the guards do not interfere."

Jean-Pierre's mind raced as Muskcobar outlined the plan. The idea was audacious, risky, and borderline insane. But it was their only chance.

THE COOKIES

That night, Jean-Pierre worked in the prison kitchen under the guise of preparing a treat for the guards—a gesture of goodwill. His hands moved with precision, each motion deliberate as he baked a batch of cookies laced with "Brugmansia", a plant rich in scopolamine notorious for its use in incapacitating victims.

As he sifted flour and stirred batter, Muskcobar stood watch near the doorway, his eyes scanning the shadows for any sign of trouble.

"Are you sure this will work?" Muskcobar asked, his voice a whisper.

Jean-Pierre glanced up; his expression grim. "If the dosage is right, they will sleep like babies. Too much, and..." He did not finish the sentence.

"We're not killers," Muskcobar said firmly.

Jean-Pierre nodded. "Exactly. Which is why I'm being careful. This is not about revenge—it's about survival."

The cookies emerged from the oven golden brown, their sweet aroma masking the dangerous secret within. Jean-Pierre packed them neatly, his heart pounding.

The next part of the plan required creativity. Muskcobar had managed to acquire dresses, wigs, and makeup through his extensive network of favors with the ladies of the night. Jean-Pierre stared at the garish attire laid out on the bed, his skepticism evident.

"Women's clothes?" he asked, holding up a sequined dress.

"Perfect disguise," Muskcobar said with a smirk. "No one's going to suspect a pair of glamorous women strolling out of here."

Jean-Pierre groaned. "You're enjoying this, aren't you?" "It reminds me of my escape from America"

"Really," Muskcobar asked.

Reluctantly, they donned the outfits, their laughter a rare moment of levity in the tense atmosphere. Muskcobar applied rouge to his cheeks with surprising finesse, while Jean-Pierre adjusted a curly blonde wig.

"Stunning," Muskcobar said, striking a pose.

Jean-Pierre rolled his eyes. "Let's just hope this works."

THE ESCAPE

When the guards gathered in the breakroom later that evening, the cookies sat invitingly on a silver tray. Their aroma filled the room, masking the dark purpose behind their creation.

"These are fancy," one guard remarked, picking one up. "Who brought them?"

Another shrugged, already biting into a cookie. "Does it matter? They are free, and they're good."

Muskcobar and Jean-Pierre, hidden in the shadows, exchanged a tense glance as the guards dug in. Laughter and banter filled the room, but it did not take long for the effects to set in.

One guard leaned back in his chair, his eyelids drooping. Another yawned loudly, rubbing his temples. Soon, their words slurred, and they began slumping over the table, one by one.

Muskcobar tilted his head toward Jean-Pierre. "It's time," he whispered.

The two men emerged from their hiding spot, now dressed in their disguises. Jean-Pierre tugged at his ill-fitting dress, muttering, "Dressed and stressed as a woman going on a date."

"Focus, a date with freedom," Muskcobar said, adjusting his wig. "We're not out yet."

Their heels clicked softly against the concrete as they made their way down the dimly lit hallway. Every sound seemed amplified in the tense silence.

A guard appeared around the corner, his cigarette glowing faintly in the darkness. He glanced at them, tipping his hat. "Good evening, ladies."

Jean-Pierre forced a high-pitched reply, "Good evening," his heart racing as they walked past. The guard came closer, Jean Pierre heart was racing, the guard caressed his butt, "I hope you come back soon I like your butt, he grinned showing some missing tooth and tobacco tinted teeth, "Buenas noches Chicas"

Once outside, they hurried toward a waiting car, where one of Muskcobar' s contacts sat behind the wheel, scanning the perimeter nervously.

"Get in," the driver hissed.

Jean-Pierre barely had time to yank off his wig before Muskcobar shoved him into the back seat.

As the car sped away from the prison gates, Muskcobar let out a triumphant laugh. "Freedom never tasted so sweet."

Jean-Pierre glanced out the window at the disappearing lights of the prison. "Let's hope it stays that way."

SAFE HAVEN

Their destination was the children's restaurant in Bogotá—a modest but bustling establishment rebuilt with grit and determination. Jacqueline and Patrick were stunned when their father and Muskcobar appeared at the back entrance, their clothes disheveled and their faces full of make-up.

"Papa?" Jacqueline exclaimed; her eyes wide open.

Patrick crossed his arms. "What have you gotten yourself into this time?"

"It's a long story," Jean-Pierre said, leaning against the wall. "But for now, we need a place to hide."

Jacqueline nodded, pulling him into a hug. "You're always welcome here, Papa. No matter what."

As they settled in, Muskcobar grinned at the siblings. "Nice place you have got here. Maybe we should consider adding a new item to the menu— 'Freedom Fries.'"

Patrick groaned. "Great. Now I have two of you to deal with."

Jean-Pierre chuckled softly, relief washing over him. For the first time in months, he felt a glimmer of hope.

14 | TRAVEL PLANS

████████G THE OPTIONS

The safe house was sparse but functional—a small apartment tucked away in Bogotá's chaotic outskirts. The peeling paint and mismatched furniture spoke of hurried preparation, but it was safe, and that was all that mattered for now.

Muskcobar lounged on a worn sofa, flipping through a tattered atlas. Jean-Pierre paced the cramped space, muttering under his breath. Patrick and Jacqueline sat at the small kitchen table, a laptop open between them, its screen glowing faintly.

"We need a plan," Jean-Pierre said, his tone sharp with urgency. "A real plan, not one of your improvised schemes, Muskcobar."

The drug lord chuckled, lighting a cigarette. "Relax, Chef. We'll figure it out. We always do."

"Not this time," Jacqueline interjected, her voice steady but firm. "The authorities will be hunting us like animals. You can't afford to stay in Colombia."

Patrick nodded; his brow furrowed. "But where do they go? Europe? Asia? The U.S. is out of the question."

Muskcobar leaned forward, exhaling a plume of smoke. "We need a place without extradition treaties. Somewhere they will not ask questions."

BRAINSTORMING DESTINATIONS

Jacqueline scrolled through a list on the laptop, her eyes flicking over country names and visa restrictions. "How about Russia? They don't extradite to most countries."

Jean-Pierre frowned, crossing his arms. "Russia? I can barely handle the cold in Bogotá. You expect me to survive a Siberian winter?"

Patrick leaned over the screen, scrolling down. "What about Venezuela? Muskcobar's contacts might still have influence there."

Muskcobar let out a dry chuckle and shook his head. "Maduro's regime is a circus on fire. One day you're safe, the next, you're on a military tribunal for blinking the wrong way. I would rather take my chances with the Vatican."

Jacqueline sighed and kept searching. "Okay, what about Southeast Asia? Thailand or Cambodia? plenty of expats. Corruption is manageable. you could disappear there."

Jean-Pierre stopped pacing and turned to her, considering the idea. "Thailand… that could work. I could find work in a restaurant—something quiet, under the radar."

Muskcobar smirked, folding his arms. "Quiet? You? I will believe it when I see it."

Patrick leaned back and stretched. "Okay, Thailand sounds promising. But how do you get there without passports that scream 'wanted fugitives?'"

Jean-Pierre rubbed his temples. "One problem at a time. First, we pick a destination. Then, we figure out how to get there."

Muskcobar raised his glass. "To a future far, far away from here."

THE CHALLENGES AHEAD

Patrick leaned back in his chair, rubbing his temples. "Even if you pick a place, how do you get there? Airports are risky. They will be watching for you."

"We don't have to go through an airport," Muskcobar said, a sly grin spreading across his face. "There are other ways to travel."

Jacqueline raised an eyebrow. "You're suggesting smuggling ourselves out, aren't you?"

"Exactly," Muskcobar replied. "I know people who can get us across borders without a passport. It's risky, but it's our best shot."

Jean-Pierre sighed, pinching the bridge of his nose. "So, we are going from cooking for criminals to becoming smugglers. Wonderful."

"Do you have a better idea?" Muskcobar shot back.

The room fell silent, the weight of the decision pressing on them. Finally, Jacqueline broke the silence. "You will need fake identities, cash, and a solid plan. This is not just about leaving Colombia—it's about starting over."

Jean Pierre nodded. "Agreed. But let's make sure we're not walking into another disaster."

A SHRED OF HOPE

The conversation lulled, the weight of their choices settling over them like a thick fog. The dimly lit room felt smaller, the walls pressing in as they realized the enormity of what lay ahead. For all their planning, their escape was still just an idea a fragile dream teetering on the edge of reality.

Jean-Pierre leaned back in his chair, exhaling slowly. Despite everything—the betrayals, the prison escape, the relentless fear of being caught—he felt something unfamiliar creeping in. Hope.

"We'll figure it out," he said, his voice steadier than he felt. "Together."

Jacqueline looked at him, searching his face for any hesitation, any sign that he didn't believe his own words. But there was none. For the first time in months, her father looked like a man with a plan, not just someone running from disaster to disaster.

Muskcobar smirked, raising his cigarette in a mock toast. "To freedom and fresh starts. May we find one before we are shot or arrested."

Patrick chuckled dryly. "Comforting."

Jacqueline sighed, shaking her head but smiling despite herself. "It's better than nothing."

For a brief moment, the tension eased. The road ahead was uncertain, riddled with dangers they had not even begun to comprehend, but for the first time in a long while, they had a direction a sliver of possibility.

Jean-Pierre looked at each of them, his ragtag group of fugitives turned family. They weren't out of danger, not even close. But if they had survived everything else, they could survive this too.

"We move at first light," he said.

No one argued. Their journey was far from over, but at least now, they had a destination.

15 | CHANGING IDENTITY

THE DECISION

The safe house in Bogotá was cramped, its peeling walls and flickering lights doing little to make their situation feel less dire. A radio crackled softly in the corner, playing an old tango, its mournful tune mirroring the weight in the room.

Patrick paced near the window, peeking through the blinds as if expecting sirens at any moment. "This isn't sustainable," he muttered. "We can't keep hiding you forever. Someone's going to recognize both of you, and then it's game over."

Muskcobar said with a smile "We need a real plan. New names, new appearances. Something that makes us untouchable."

220

Jean-Pierre sat in the only decent chair, rubbing his temples. "New names alone won't be enough. We need to become different people."

Muskcobar exhaled a cloud of smoke from his cigar, lounging against the kitchen counter like they were discussing vacation plans. "Ah, mes amis, now you're thinking like survivors. But names and passports? That's amateur hour. If we truly want to vanish, we need the full package."

Patrick stopped pacing. "And what's that supposed to mean?"

Muskcobar grinned. "Plastic surgery."

Jacqueline's nose wrinkled. "You can't be serious."

"Oh, but I am," Muskcobar said, spreading his arms theatrically. "Think about it. The world's most infamous people don't just hide. They become someone else."

Patrick scoffed. "That's insane."

Muskcobar flicked ash into the sink. "What's insane is thinking you'll make it out of an airport with that face." He pointed at Jean-Pierre. "You? You're too well-known. If someone sees you, poof—extradition. Me? I have a certain... reputation. A new face means a new life."

Jean-Pierre leaned forward. "And who do you know that can do this?"

Muskcobar smirked. "I know the best plastic surgeon."

Jean Pierre shook his head. "No way. I'm not slicing up my face because you think it's the only option."

"You don't have to," Muskcobar said, rolling his wrist dismissively. "Patrick and Jacqueline stay here, a haircut, different clothes, new passports— you'll be fine. But Jean-Pierre and I? We need... modifications."

Jacqueline folded her arms. "I don't like it."

Jean-Pierre sighed. "I don't like it either, ma fille. But if we want to survive, we don't have a choice."

Muskcobar raised his glass of Aguardiente "To re incarnation."

Jean-Pierre hesitated, then clinked his glass against Muskcobar' s. Patrick and Jacqueline exchanged a look before raising their own.

"To re incarnation," they echoed.

THE PLASTIC SURGEON'S OFFICE

The clinic was discreet, tucked away in a quiet, affluent neighborhood. From the outside, it looked like an upscale dental office, but inside, the pristine white halls and state-of-the-art equipment spoke to something far more specialized.

Dr. Cardoza greeted them with the air of a man who had seen—and changed—many faces. His salt-and-pepper hair was slicked back, his suit crisp, his smile calculated.

"Welcome," he said, shaking Muskcobar' s hand. "I understand you're looking for… transformation."

Muskcobar grinned. "Doctor, my friend here and I need to become ghosts."

Dr. Cardoza arched an eyebrow. "How drastic?"

Muskcobar gestured toward Jean-Pierre. "For him? Subtle. Familiar, but not too familiar. If an old friend passes him on the street, they should hesitate. For me?" He smirked. "I want to be reborn. Younger. Sharper. Presidential."

Patrick snorted. "Oh, for God's sake."

Dr. Cardoza chuckled. "Subtle changes are often the most effective." He motioned for them to sit, tapping on his tablet. "Let's take a look at what we can do."

The large screen displayed digital mock-ups.

Jean-Pierre's brows furrowed as he studied his altered face—his nose slightly thinner, jawline subtly refined, crow's feet smoothed out. "It's still me," he murmured. "Just… different."

"Precisely," Dr. Cardoza said. "Familiarity without recognition."

Muskcobar, on the other hand, admired his new face like a sculptor inspecting a masterpiece. "Ah! Magnifique. A face fit for history books."

Patrick rolled his eyes. "You mean Interpol's most wanted list?"

Dr. Cardoza ignored the jab. "If you're satisfied, we can begin in a few weeks."

The Ex President nodded. "Let's do it."

LEARNING TO BLEND

Their transformation wasn't just physical. Muskcobar insisted that if they were going to survive, they needed to become their new identities.

We try Brazil. Brazil has reluctance to extradite for political persecution and the President can be bribed easily the Reals is very low that will be cheap, if Lula is in power that will be easy if Bolsonaro comes back, it will even be easier.

"However, you don't just look Brazilian," he declared, pacing the small living room of their safe house. "You need to live Brazilian. You breathe the culture, eat the food, dance the samba. If someone asks you where you were born, your answer should roll off your tongue like you have lived there your whole life."

Jean Pierre sighed, rubbing his temples. "And I suppose you already have the perfect plan to make that happen?"

Muskcobar grinned. "Of course. Language classes, cooking, dancing—the whole experience."

That's how they found themselves crammed into a brightly lit classroom in a language school, surrounded by posters of Brazilian landscapes and vocabulary charts. The room smelled of old books and cheap coffee. A warm, enthusiastic instructor, a middle-aged woman named Clara, stood at the front, beaming at her new students.

"Bom dia," she greeted, clapping her hands together. "Repeat after me: Bom dia!"

"Bom dia," Jean Pierre repeated smoothly, her natural knack for languages shining through.

The instructor chuckled. "Very close, Jean Pierre. Let's try it again."

Jean-Pierre sat up straight, clearing his throat. "Eu gosto de cozinhar."

His thick French accent mangled the words so badly that Clara physically winced.

She recovered quickly, nodding encouragingly. "Close enough! You just said, 'I like cooking.' That's good!"

Jacqueline smirked. "Papa, you've been saying that since I was born."

From the back of the room, Muskcobar leaned lazily against the wall, watching the group struggle. "Language is important," he admitted with a smirk, "but trust me—in Brazil, charm and confidence open more doors than perfect grammar."

Clara arched an eyebrow, unimpressed. "Boa sorte com isso," she muttered.

Jacqueline leaned toward Patrick. "What did she just say?"

"She said, 'Good luck with that.'"

Patrick shook his head. "I think she meant, 'You're doomed.'"

Muskcobar merely grinned. "Luck is for people without charisma."

The lesson continued, but progress was slow. Jean Pierre kept confusing words, and over-pronounced syllables, Muskcobar, to no one's surprise, barely tried.

After an hour of struggle, Clara finally sighed. "Maybe we should take a break."

Jean Pierre slumped in his chair. "God bless you, woman."

As the class ended, Muskcobar clapped Jean Pierre on the back. "Relax, my friend. You don't have to speak like a Brazilian to be Brazilian."

Jean Pierre groaned. "Oh yeah ? Then what do I need?" Muskcobar winked. "A little more rhythm."

CULINARY TRAINING AND
SAMBA LESSONS

Jean-Pierre threw himself into learning Brazilian cuisine, transforming their safe house kitchen into a training ground. Every available surface was covered with bowls of fresh herbs, sacks of black beans, and cuts of pork waiting to be slow-cooked to perfection. The rich, smoky aroma of simmering feijoada filled the air, making the cramped kitchen feel like a bustling Brazilian eatery.

Patrick walked in, sniffing the air. "Smells amazing. What is it?"

Jean-Pierre, sweat glistening on his brow, stirred a heavy pot. "Feijoada," he declared proudly. "A classic Brazilian stew. Beans, pork, spices—comfort food."

Patrick grabbed a spoon and took a cautious bite. His eyes widened. "Okay, I'll admit it. This is good."

Jacqueline leaned over the counter, plucking a piece of crispy pork from a nearby plate. "Papa, I think this might be the best thing you've ever made."

Jean-Pierre smirked. "That's because I finally understand the secret."

Muskcobar, lounging by the window with a glass of rum, raised an eyebrow. "And what's that?"

Jean-Pierre lifted a wooden spoon dramatically. "Brazilian food isn't about precision—it's about passion."

Muskcobar chuckled. "Good. Now apply that same logic to dancing, because you all move like broken marionettes."

And so began the samba lessons.

The dance studio was small, its wooden floor polished to a shine. A large mirror lined the front wall, reflecting the skeptical faces of the group as their instructor, a fiery woman named Valeria, clapped her hands to get their attention.

"Tango is for lovers. Salsa is for seduction," she announced. "But samba? Samba is joy. If you cannot feel the music, you cannot be Brazilian."

Jean-Pierre shifted uncomfortably. "I cook. I do not dance."

Valeria ignored him and signaled the drummer in the corner. The fast-paced beat of samba music filled the room, vibrant and infectious.

"Step, sway, turn!" she commanded.

Jean-Pierre attempted to follow, but his movements were stiff, awkward. He tripped over his own feet, nearly toppling into Muskcobar. "Mon dieu! How do people make this look easy?"

Patrick groaned from the back. "I think I pulled something."

Jacqueline, on the other hand, twirled effortlessly, her movements fluid and natural. "Looks like I'm the only one with rhythm," she teased.

Muskcobar, unsurprisingly, was a natural. He moved with ease, his steps precise, his body in sync with the music. With a flourish, he spun Jacqueline and dipped her dramatically, flashing a grin at the others.

"You have to feel the music, my friends!" he declared.

Jean-Pierre shot him a glare. "Someone is chasing us."

Muskcobar shrugged. "Then let's hope they can't dance.

FRUSTRATION AND DETERMINATION

Despite their best efforts, blending in as Brazilians proved far more difficult than they had imagined. Language lessons left them tongue-tied, Jean-Pierre's feijoada was still missing the authentic touch, and their samba moves looked more like an awkward shuffle than a rhythmic dance.

One evening, they collapsed around the dinner table, exhaustion settling in like a heavy fog. The dim glow of the kitchen light flickered slightly, casting long shadows over their worn-out faces.

Patrick let out a long sigh, pushing his plate away. "This isn't working," he muttered. "You 'll never pass as locals."

"You are trying. That has to count for something."

Jean-Pierre, nursing a cup of strong Brazilian coffee, leaned back in his chair. "It's not about perfection," he said, rubbing his temple. "It's about staying under the radar. Nobody is expecting us to be fluent overnight."

Muskcobar, ever the optimist, swirled his rum in his glass before raising it in the air. "Failure," he declared, "is just a step on the road to greatness."

Jean-Pierre snorted. "And how many steps until we get there?"

Muskcobar smirked. "Just enough to keep things interesting."

With weary but determined expressions, they clinked their glasses together. The toast was silent but meaningful.

Outside, the sounds of a distant samba band drifted through the warm night air. The city was alive, indifferent to their struggles. They weren't Brazilian yet. But they were getting closer.

16 | FROM SAMBIA TO TANGO

The transition from the rhythmic, vibrant world of samba to the dramatic elegance of tango marked another chapter in their journey of reinvention. Muskcobar had a new plan: if Brazil didn't work, perhaps Argentina would. "We need options," he declared one evening over a dinner of Brazilian feijóada. "And if we're going to pass as Argentinians, we must sound the part—and move like it too."

The group exchanged skeptical glances, but the logic was undeniable.

"Argentina extradition can be denied for political persecution and the Argentinian Pesos is very low, they have that Kichner legacy and Panama Papers legacy that should be easy, Milei might be more difficult to bribe but he hates Maduro as much as I do"

MASTERING THE ACCENT

Their first challenge was the Argentine accent. At a local language school, the instructor, a wiry man named Alejandro with sharp features and a knack for mimicry, wasted no time diving into the nuances of Argentine Spanish.

"First," Alejandro said, pacing the room, "you must forget everything you know about pronouncing your S's and L's. Here, the 'y' and 'll' are like 'zh' in pleasure. Say, Yo me llamo Jacqueline."

"Zho meh zhamo Jacqueline," Jacqueline repeated, her natural linguistic talent shining through.

"Not bad," Alejandro said, nodding approvingly. "You've got potential."

"Now you, Patrick," Alejandro said, gesturing to him.

Patrick frowned, his brow furrowing as he focused. "Zho meh zhamo Patrick.

Alejandro winced, holding up a hand. "Stop. You sound like a drunken tourist who just stumbled out of a tango bar. Loosen your jaw. Try again."

Jean Pierre sighed and gave it another shot, his pronunciation marginally better. Alejandro squinted at him, tilting his head. "It's... progress."

Jean-Pierre, meanwhile, sat stiffly in his chair, his arms crossed. When his turn came, he cleared his throat, his French accent immediately taking control. "Zho meh zhamo Jean-Pierre," he said, the words sounding as though they had been dipped in Bordeaux and rolled in baguettes.

Alejandro groaned, dragging a hand down his face. "Mon dieu," Jean-Pierre muttered under his breath, earning a sharp look from the instructor.

"Don't worry, Jean-Pierre," Alejandro said, smirking. "Argentinians are dramatic. Just wave your hands a lot—it distracts from the pronunciation."

Muskcobar, leaning casually against the wall, chuckled. "Perfect advice for a politician. You're already halfway there, Chef."

Alejandro's eyes flicked to Muskcobar. "And you? Would you like to try?"

Muskcobar straightened, his confidence unshaken. "Zho meh zhamo... El Maestro," he said, his voice dripping with theatrical flair.

Jacqueline burst out laughing, while Patrick rolled his eyes. Alejandro raised an unimpressed eyebrow. "I see you have already mastered the art of arrogance. Now let us work on your vowels."

The lessons continued with Alejandro barking instructions and correcting mistakes. The group wrestled with the subtleties of the Argentine drawl, each struggling in their own way.

Patrick grumbled as Alejandro made him repeat a sentence for the tenth time. "Why can't we just learn regular Spanish? This feels like overkill."

"Because," Alejandro said, his voice sharp, "regular Spanish will make you stand out in Buenos Aires. Trust me, you do not want to stand out."

Jacqueline picked up the accent quickly, her musical ear allowing her to mimic the instructor's intonation almost perfectly. "How am I doing?" she asked after practicing a particularly long phrase.

Alejandro clapped his hands together, smiling for the first time. "Jacqueline, you sound like you were born in Recoleta. Excellent."

Patrick groaned. "Great, now she's the teacher's pet."

Jacqueline smirked. "It's not my fault I'm talented, hermano."

Jean-Pierre, however, remained the most challenged. Alejandro sighed as the older man once again butchered a simple phrase. "Your French is fighting you every step of the way," the instructor said.

"I'm aware," Jean-Pierre replied, exasperated. "Do you think I like sounding like a bad impression of myself?"

"Patience, Chef," Muskcobar interjected, his grin widening. "You have mastered soufflés. Surely you can master this."

Alejandro, despite his initial frustration, softened as the lessons progressed. "You're improving," he said to Jean-Pierre after an hour. "Slowly but improving."

By the end of the session, the group was exhausted but slightly more confident. Alejandro handed out practice sheets, warning them that perfection would not come overnight.

"Keep practicing," he said firmly. "If you want to survive in Argentina, your accent must be impeccable. One slip, and people will notice."

As they left the classroom, Muskcobar clapped Jean-Pierre on the shoulder. "Cheer up, my friend. By the time we are done, you'll be able to charm the tango clubs of Buenos Aires with nothing but your voice."

Jean-Pierre snorted. "If they don't laugh me off the stage first."

The others chuckled; their spirits buoyed despite the challenges ahead. Each lesson brought them closer to their goal, one syllable at a time.

LESSONS ON THE DANCE FLOOR

The second part of their training was learning tango, the soul of Argentine culture. The dance studio, with its polished wooden floors and mirrors reflecting flickering candlelight, felt like stepping into another world. Their instructor, a statuesque woman named Valeria, exuded both grace and an unyielding authority.

She clapped her hands sharply, silencing the nervous shuffling of feet. "Tango is not just a dance," Valeria declared, her voice carrying through the room like the opening note of a symphony. "It is a conversation. It is passion. It is life. You do not just move—you feel."

With a flourish, she demonstrated a simple step, her movements fluid and precise. Her feet seemed to glide across the floor as though carried by the music itself. Then she turned sharply to Jean-Pierre, who stood awkwardly near the edge of the room, attempting to avoid her gaze.

"You," she said, pointing to him. "Come."

Jean-Pierre froze, then reluctantly stepped forward. "Lead me," Valeria instructed, taking his hands and positioning them properly. Her gaze pierced through him.

Jean-Pierre hesitated; his movements stiff as he tried to mimic her steps. He was too focused on counting in his head to notice her growing impatience. Valeria stopped him abruptly, her stern expression softening into faint amusement. "No, no. Tango is not about thinking. It is about instinct, connection, feeling."

Jean-Pierre let out a frustrated sigh. "I am a chef," he replied dryly. "My instincts are for soufflés, not samba."

"Tango," Valeria corrected, pulling him into position again. "Now, move."

As the music began again, Jean-Pierre stumbled through a series of awkward steps, his face set in a grimace. Valeria guided him firmly, her own steps never faltering. "Relax," she murmured. "The dance does not demand perfection. It demands presence."

Meanwhile, Jacqueline glided across the floor with surprising ease. She caught on quickly, her natural grace lending itself to the rhythm of the music. "It's like a conversation," she mused aloud, stepping confidently with her partner. "You just have to listen to what the other person is saying."

Patrick, in contrast, was a disaster. He tripped over his own feet twice before nearly colliding with Valeria mid-step. She caught him with a sharp glare and steadied him with a firm grip.

"This is impossible," Patrick muttered, throwing his hands up in exasperation.

"Impossible?" Valeria said, raising an eyebrow. "Do you think Messi gave up after missing his first goal? Tango is a discipline, a commitment. If you want to master it, you must give yourself fully to it."

Muskcobar, as always, seemed to glide effortlessly. He partnered with one of the assistants, twirling her with dramatic flair. "See?" he said, spinning Jacqueline when it was his turn. "It's all about confidence."

"Easy for you to say," Patrick grumbled, narrowly avoiding another stumble.

Valeria clapped again, signaling for the group to switch partners. Jacqueline partnered with her father, guiding him gently through the steps. "Papa, stop thinking so hard," she teased. "You're holding on like I'm a bag of flour."

Jean-Pierre chuckled despite himself. "Well, you are light on your feet."

When Patrick partnered with Valeria again, she pushed him harder, making him repeat the same steps until they were etched into his muscle memory. "Again," she barked as he tripped over her foot. "And this time, do not look at your feet. Look at me."

The night wore on, the group's confidence growing incrementally with each round of the music. By the end, even Patrick managed a clumsy but serviceable turn that earned a small nod of approval from Valeria.

"You are all... works in progress," she said, her tone begrudgingly complimentary. "But progress nonetheless."

As they left the studio, their bodies sore and their spirits buoyed by the triumph of surviving Valeria's intensity, Muskcobar turned to the group with a grin. "See? The tango isn't so bad. Now all we need is an audience."

"An audience?" Jean-Pierre asked, his brow furrowing.

Muskcobar winked. "What's the point of learning if you don't perform?"

Jacqueline groaned. "Let's get through the lessons first, Maestro."

Despite the challenges, there was a spark of excitement in their eyes. Tango was not just a dance; it was their way of stepping closer to reinvention.

FRUSTRATION AND PROGRESS

Despite their initial struggles, the group began to find their footing—quite literally. Each session brought small improvements, their awkward, disjointed movements gradually giving way to something resembling rhythm. Patrick, who had once seemed destined to trip over every step, finally managed a respectable ocho cortado after hours of practice.

"You see?" Valeria said, clapping her hands. "Even the most stubborn feet can learn to move with grace."

Patrick rolled his eyes, though a faint smile tugged at his lips. "It only took a hundred tries."

"It took perseverance," Valeria corrected, turning her attention to Jacqueline, who was executing a flawless gancho. "Now this is how you command a room."

Jacqueline grinned, her movements confident and fluid. "It's all about listening, right? You always said tango is a conversation.

Jean-Pierre, on the other hand, still looked as though he were at war with his own feet. "It's more like an argument," he muttered after stumbling for the third time during a giro.

"Papa, you're overthinking it," Jacqueline teased, coming to his side. She placed her hands on his shoulders and adjusted his stance. "Relax. Feel the music, not the steps."

Jean-Pierre sighed but followed her lead. For a moment, he moved with surprising fluidity, the tension in his posture easing. But then his foot caught on hers, and they stumbled together, laughter breaking the seriousness of the moment.

"You, see?" Muskcobar said, watching from the corner as he wiped his brow. "Tango is the perfect metaphor for life. You stumble, you recover, and you keep moving. Add a little flair, and everyone thinks it was intentional."

"Is that your secret?" Patrick asked, raising an eyebrow.

"Among many," Muskcobar replied with a sly grin.

As the evening wore on, the group began to tire. After a particularly grueling session, they collapsed onto the studio floor, their sweat-soaked shirts sticking to their backs. The wooden planks felt cool against their skin as they stared at the ceiling, catching their breath.

"This might actually work," Jacqueline said, her smile wide as she stared at the softly glowing chandelier above.

Jean-Pierre shook his head, dabbing his forehead with a towel. "I wouldn't call it 'working' just yet," he said, though there was a hint of pride in his voice.

"Small victories, Papa," Jacqueline teased, nudging him playfully.

Muskcobar raised his water bottle in a mock toast. "To tango," he declared. "Proof that even the uncoordinated can become elegant with enough practice—and determination."

They clinked their bottles together, the sound echoing softly in the empty studio. In that moment, their shared laughter and camaraderie felt like a balm for the chaos surrounding them.

They were far from mastering their new identities, but with every step—every stumble—they inched closer to the lives they were fighting to rebuild.

Every day, they trained. Every day, they practiced their steps, their accents, their identities. And all the while, the bodyguards watched in stunned disbelief, shaking their heads in utter confusion. Jean Pierre was even experiencing Argentinian recipes.

Choripán: A popular street food, choripán is a grilled chorizo sausage served in a crusty bread roll with chimichurri sauce.

Carbonada: A rich stew made with meat, potatoes, sweet corn, carrots, and sometimes dried fruits, typically cooked in a hollowed-out pumpkin.

Humita: A dish made from corn dough, wrapped in corn husks and steamed or boiled.

What had they become? The day had finally arrived—the day Jean Pierre Labaguette could no longer run.

The Plastic surgery clinic smelled sterile, but beneath the surface was something darker. A place where men buried their pasts under new skin.

Jean Pierre stood stiffly as the surgeon laid out a catalog of faces before him. Rows of strangers, lifeless and blank, stared back. Each face could be his. Each one could erase the man he was.

"Choose one, or I'll choose for you," Muskcobar growled from the corner of the room. His patience had thinned to nothing.

Jean Pierre forced a smirk, but it barely held. "What about you? Already picked yours, Muskcobar?"

Muskcobar' s eyes flashed dangerously. "If I change my face, Jean Pierre, you and the rest of the team will never know what it looks like. Not even for a second."

Jean Pierre stiffened. "Why should mine be any different?"

"Because I *pay* for yours." Muskcobar' s voice dropped into a low, menacing rasp. "I don't need you, Jean Pierre. Don't start acting like a diva now. Pick. I'll see it."

Jean Pierre's gaze dropped back to the catalog, his heart pounding louder than the ticking clock. He traced the faces with his fingertips, each one feeling like a silent death. Finally, he pointed.

"This one."

Muskcobar leaned in, glancing briefly at the chosen face. "Good. You'll look decent enough at customs."

Jean Pierre was silent as they led him to the surgical room. The fluorescent lights above felt colder than ice. A nurse handed him a set of patient scrubs.

The surgeon approached, holding a syringe with a practiced calm. "Relax," the surgeon said, his voice soothing but distant. "You'll be under before you know it." "In a few days you will look younger and Argentinian" "except for the arrogance" he added.

Jean Pierre's hand shot out faster than thought. He seized the syringe, twisting it effortlessly in his palm. Before the surgeon could react, Jean Pierre plunged the needle into his neck. The man's eyes widened in shock, then fluttered shut as he collapsed.

The nurse gasped, but Jean Pierre was already on her. His eyes, fierce and unwavering, silenced her before she could scream.

"Get on the table," he ordered coldly.

Trembling, she obeyed. Jean Pierre tied her wrists and ankles swiftly, securing her to the operating table.

He slipped into the surgeon's white coat, adjusting the collar with a glance in the mirror. He pulled down the mask just enough to reveal a smirk.

Jean Pierre Labaguette was no one's puppet.

The clinic's automatic doors slid open, and Jean Pierre stepped onto the street. His steps were calm, measured.

A taxi cruised by. He flagged it down.

"US Consulate. *Fast.*"

The cabbie didn't ask questions. The danger was too obvious.

Entering the consulate wasn't easy. Security guards hesitated. His disguise, though convincing, raised eyebrows. But Jean Pierre had one final weapon.

His *story.*

He spun a tale so wild, so extravagant, that even the guards exchanged uncertain glances. Soon, word reached the DEA. Whispers followed. Jean Pierre was ushered through a back door, the weight of his reputation pulling him forward.

Inside, the US consul's office was dimly lit. The consul leaned back in his chair, staring at the infamous man across from him.

"Stay here for a few days," the consul said after a long pause. "Let the heat die down. I'll think of something."

Jean Pierre exhaled for the first time in hours. "Thank you," he said, voice cracking with exhaustion. "Can I... can I stay in the kitchen? Cook for you and your staff?"

The consul arched an eyebrow. "You want to cook?"

Jean Pierre's smile returned tired, but genuine. "I'm better in a kitchen." The atmosphere was tense at the U.S. Embassy in Bogotá. The Colombian government was determined to bring Jean Pierre to justice. To make matters worse, Muskcobar had placed a bounty on his head, and, adding insult to injury, Jean Pierre couldn't find all the ingredients he needed for his cooking.

However, the embassy staff found a silver lining. Jean Pierre's culinary skills had transformed their daily meals, and his exotic flavors were a welcome distraction from the tension outside.

SUBMARINE MISSION

One afternoon, the ambassador called Jean Pierre into his office.

"Jean Pierre, the situation is complicated," the ambassador began, leaning back in his chair. "But I have to say, your food has been the highlight of my day. I may have found a solution to get you out of the country." "But you will need to become a special agent".

Jean Pierre raised an eyebrow. "A solution? I'm no James Bond, Ambassador."

"I can arrange for you to leave the country on a submarine," the ambassador replied calmly.

Jean Pierre blinked. "A submarine? To where?"

"It's a classified mission. You'd be tasked with escorting someone from a Caribbean island back to the U.S. to face justice."

Jean Pierre shook his head. "No, no, no. I'm done cruising the Caribbean. Another narco, I presume?"

The ambassador gave a faint smile. "A high-level politician involved in the narco world."

Jean Pierre sighed. "Like so many others. Sorry, Ambassador, but I'm not interested."

Time passed, and the Colombian government's pursuit seemed to ease. The protests in front of the embassy dwindled. Jean Pierre thought he might have a chance at a quieter life.

A month later, the ambassador summoned him again. This time, the meeting took place in a dimly lit room with tinted windows. On the other side of the glass, a young woman sat, speaking with immigration officers. She was beautiful, her eyes filled with fear.

The ambassador watched Jean Pierre's reaction closely. "You know her?"

Jean Pierre nodded, his throat tightening. "Yes. That's Sandra. She's a friend."

"She's applying for a visa," the ambassador said. "But given her past, there's no chance she'll get it. Muskcobar wants her dead."

Jean Pierre's heart sank. "She's not a bad person. She just got caught up with the wrong people."

"Do you want to help her?" the ambassador asked quietly.

Jean Pierre's eyes remained fixed on Sandra, who was now wiping away tears.

"Yes. I want to help her."

The ambassador nodded. "Then take the mission. She'll go with you. If you succeed, she'll get permanent residency and possibly witness protection."

Jean Pierre inhaled deeply. Memories of his time with Sandra flooded back—the love, the passion, the laughter. He turned to the ambassador, extended his hand, and shook it firmly.

"I'll do it. Who is this narco-politician?"

The ambassador smiled. "You'll find out soon enough. Get ready. You and Sandra—that is her name, correct?"

Jean Pierre nodded. "Yes, Sandra."

"Both of you will leave soon. One more thing," the ambassador added with a sly grin. "There's a small kitchen on the submarine."

Jean Pierre chuckled. "Very small, I suppose.

The submarine journey was anything but pleasant. The entire team of Navy SEALs had Latin American backgrounds, carefully selected to blend in as sicarios and drug smugglers.

"You have a French accent," one of them said, narrowing his eyes at Jean Pierre.

"No," another chimed in. "That's Argentinian."

The tallest SEAL smirked. "I'd swear you were our ex-president who fled to France."

Laughter echoed through the tight quarters. "Right, Tom. An ex-president on a DEA mission, deep in a submarine."

Sandra smiled, squeezing Jean Pierre's hand beneath the table.

After days beneath the ocean, they finally surfaced near Tortuga, the infamous Haitian island once a pirate stronghold. The submarine anchored in a concealed underwater cave just off the coast.

17 | THE DARIEN GAP

A Few weeks before Jean Pierre submarine trip

INTO THE JUNGLE

The jungle swallowed Muskcobar and Sylvie who had escaped from Bogota. A damp, green world of twisting vines and towering trees closed in around them, suffocating in its intensity. The thick, waxy leaves overhead formed a near-solid canopy, allowing only fractured beams of sunlight to stab through the darkness like golden knives. The air was dense, heavy with moisture, and carried the rich, rotten scent of decay.

Each step was a battle. The mud sucked at their boots, pulling them down with a relentless grip, while fallen branches and tangled roots threatened to trip them at every turn. Sylvie swatted at a mosquito that had found its way to his neck, only to feel another bite at his wrist. The jungle wasn't just alive, it was hungry.

Ahead, Esteban their guide moved like a ghost, his feet barely making a sound as he sliced through the dense undergrowth with his machete. Every movement was precise, economical, a man at home in the chaos of nature.

Sylvie, in contrast, was not. Her shirt clung to his body, drenched with sweat, and her lungs burned with each labored breath. "Tell me again," she said, swiping at a vine that wrapped around his arm like a living thing, "why the hell you didn't go to Brazil or Argentina with bribes.

Muskcobar let out a low chuckle. "Bribes only work when there's someone to pay off. Here? Money won't save you from a jaguar, a snake, or a guerrilla with an itchy trigger finger." He flicked the ash from his cigar, seemingly unfazed by the hellscape surrounding them.

"I need to find Jean Pierre and kill him"

Esteban halted suddenly, his hand snapping up. The group stopped immediately, senses on high alert.

Sylvie followed Esteban's gaze to the forest floor, where a thick, coiled shape lay motionless among the fallen leaves. His stomach tightened. A fer-de-lance, one of the most venomous snakes in the Americas.

Muskcobar whistled low under his breath. "Well, that's a problem."

Sylvie didn't move. His entire body was locked in place, waiting, barely breathing. The snake's scaled body was as thick as his forearm, its triangular head barely visible beneath the coils.

Esteban took a slow step forward, raising his machete, and in one swift motion, brought the blade down. The jungle exploded in a blur of movement as the snake uncoiled violently, thrashing as its severed head snapped uselessly at the air. Blood splattered the ground, mixing with the damp earth.

Sylvie exhaled sharply. "Jesus."

Esteban nudged the now-limp body with his boot, ensuring it was truly dead before wiping his blade on a broad leaf. "Stay alert," he murmured. "The jungle is always watching."

Muskcobar took a long drag from his cigar, exhaling slowly. "I like this guy," he muttered. "Knows how to handle himself."

Sylvie wasn't sure if Muskcobar was talking about Esteban—or the snake.

They pressed on, moving deeper into the jungle's embrace. Every step felt like trespassing into a world that did not belong to them. Around them, unseen creatures moved in the shadows, their eyes glowing faintly in the half-light. The calls of howler monkeys rang through the trees, an eerie, guttural sound that sent shivers down Sylvie's spine.

Then, Esteban stopped again—this time, his expression serious. He raised a hand, signaling for silence.

A rustling noise, barely perceptible, carried through the thick foliage. Then, voices. Low murmurs in

Spanish. Rough laughter. The sound of weapons shifting.

Sylvie's pulse quickened.

Muskcobar' s casual stance didn't change, but his hand drifted toward his pistol. "Guerrillas?" he whispered.

Esteban didn't answer. He crouched low, motioning for them to do the same.

Sylvie followed suit, her breath shallow. She could make out the faint glow of a cigarette through the trees, the orange ember flaring each time its owner inhaled.

They stayed frozen, unmoving. The voices drifted closer.

Then—silence.

No footsteps. No rustling.

Nothing.

Sylvie could feel the sweat dripping down his spine, the way the jungle itself seemed to hold its breath.

Then, finally, the voices resumed, fading back into the depths of the jungle.

Esteban remained still for a long moment before giving a single nod. "Move," he whispered. "Quietly."

Muskcobar let out a slow breath, shaking his head with a smirk. "Welcome to the Darién," he muttered under his breath. "Where the trees have eyes, and the wrong step gets you killed."

"I wanted to build an highway from Colombia to Panama, if only I could have been the President a but longer"

Sylvie swallowed hard, gripping the straps of his backpack. There was no turning back now.

THE RIVER CROSSING

By midday, the jungle felt like an oven, the air thick and unmoving. Every breath was labored, the humidity pressing down on them like an unseen hand. Mosquitoes swarmed in dense clouds, their relentless buzzing mixing with the distant, echoing calls of unseen creatures. Sylvie's shirt was drenched, sticking to his back as he swatted at the insects, his patience running thin.

When they finally stumbled into a clearing, the sight before them sent a fresh wave of dread washing over him—a wide, fast-moving river, its dark waters churning violently as it cut through the landscape like a scar.

Sylvie exhaled sharply. "Tell me we're not swimming across that."

Esteban, unfazed, shrugged off his pack and pulled out a coil of rope. "One by one," he said, his voice calm but firm. "You follow my steps exactly. Keep your eyes forward, don't fight the current." He tied the rope around his waist and motioned for them to do the same.

Muskcobar clapped Sylvie on the back, his grin maddeningly intact. "After you, Love."

Sylvie shot him a glare but said nothing. She stepped forward, gripping the rope tightly as she followed Esteban into the water. The moment he stepped in, the current hit like a truck. The cold was a shock at first, a brief relief from the suffocating heat, but the force of the river was far worse. It clawed at his legs, trying to pull him under, each step more treacherous than the last.

Halfway across, his boot slipped on a slick rock, and suddenly, the world tilted. His balance vanished, and the river yanked him downward in an instant.

Panic surged as water rushed over his head, filling his ears with a deafening roar. His limbs flailed instinctively, grasping for something—anything— to hold onto.

Then, just as suddenly, a hand clamped around his forearm, strong and unyielding.

Muskcobar.

He steadied Sylvie with an effortless grip, his other hand still holding onto the rope. "No drowning allowed, my love," he said with a smirk, pulling Sylvie upright.

Sylvie coughed out a mouthful of river water, her heart pounding in her chest. "Go to hell," she muttered, gripping the rope tighter.

Muskcobar only laughed.

The last few steps felt like an eternity, but finally, Sylvie's boots hit solid ground. She collapsed onto the muddy bank, his breath coming in short, ragged gasps.

Esteban smirked as he watched them. "That was the easy part."

Muskcobar stretched, wringing out his soaked shirt. "I do hope the 'hard part' doesn't involve man-eating fish."

Esteban merely gestured ahead. "Keep moving."

Sylvie groaned, dragging himself to her feet. Her body ached, but she knew better than to waste time complaining. The jungle was merciless. It wouldn't wait for them to recover.

And so, with their clothes heavy and dripping, they trudged forward, deeper into the unknown.

A NIGHT IN THE JUNGLE

By nightfall, the jungle had changed.

The oppressive heat of the day had given way to something worse—an eerie, suffocating stillness. The air, once thick with the scent of wet earth and decay, now carried something sharper, more primal. The darkness was absolute, pressing in from all sides, swallowing the trees, the sky, even their own breaths.

The sounds had shifted too. The chattering of birds had fallen silent, replaced by the deep, guttural calls of unseen predators. A distant growl sent a shiver down Sylvie's spine.

Esteban built a small fire, the flickering glow barely cutting through the blackness. He crouched beside it, sharpening his machete with slow, deliberate strokes. "We sleep in shifts," he said. "Never all at once."

Sylvie sat close to the fire, absently poking at the embers with a stick. Her muscles ached, exhaustion gnawing at her, but she knew better than to let her guard down.

Muskcobar lounged nearby, chewing on the end of his cigar, though he hadn't bothered to light it. He watched the flames, his expression unreadable.

"Do you think I will find him?" Muskcobar asked suddenly, breaking the silence.

Sylvie didn't look at him. "Do we have a choice?"

Muskcobar exhaled slowly. "There's always a choice."

Sylvie let out a dry chuckle, shaking her head. "He abandoned me"

Muskcobar tilted his head, considering this. "You sound like someone who's already accepted the ending to her own story, you still love him"

Sylvie didn't respond.

Taking first watch, she sat rigid, knife in hand, ears straining for the slightest sign of movement beyond the fire's reach. The jungle hummed around them—alive, waiting.

Somewhere in the distance, something howled.

Muskcobar shifted but didn't sit up. "That didn't sound friendly."

Sylvie tightened his grip on the knife. "Nothing in this place is."

The hours stretched long, broken only by the occasional snap of a distant branch, the rustle of something moving just beyond sight. When Muskcobar eventually nudged him, Sylvie barely hesitated before handing over the watch.

She lay down on the hard earth, her body screaming for rest. The damp ground was cold beneath her, but exhaustion overpowered discomfort.

As his eyes fluttered shut, the jungle whispered around her, its presence never fading. Even in sleep, he knew—She was being watched.

THE FINAL PUSH

By the third day, their bodies screamed for rest. Every step was agony, their muscles stiff with exhaustion, their throats raw from dehydration. The jungle had drained them—physically, mentally, completely. Their rations were nearly gone, their clothes clung to them in damp, filth-streaked patches, and the constant hum of insects had become an unbearable symphony of torment.

Sylvie's legs felt like lead as he trudged forward, her breath coming in short, ragged bursts. Her boots sank into the soft earth with every step, the mud sucking at them like it wanted to claim him whole.

Ahead, Esteban moved with the silent precision of a predator. Unlike them, he showed no signs of fatigue. If anything, he seemed more alert, his sharp eyes scanning the dense foliage, reading the jungle in ways they never could.

Muskcobar, despite his usual bravado, was quieter now. His usual cocky smirk had been replaced with a look of tight concentration. He wasn't invincible here, and he knew it.

Then, suddenly, Esteban raised a fist.

They froze.

Sylvie followed his gaze and felt his stomach drop.

Up ahead, half-hidden by thick undergrowth, a group of armed men moved through the trees.

Guerrillas.

Muskcobar' s hand drifted toward his gun.

Esteban shook his head once. Not yet.

Sylvie swallowed hard, her fingers tightening around the straps of his pack. Her pulse thundered in his ears as the Spanish voices drifted closer—low murmurs, occasional bursts of laughter, the distinct metallic clink of rifles shifting against their shoulders.

They crouched low, barely breathing. Sylvie felt the damp earth press against her palms as she steadied himself. Every muscle in his body screamed to run, but he knew better. One wrong move, one snapped twig, and they were dead.

The seconds dragged.

The men passed, their voices growing fainter, their boots crunching against the jungle floor. Then— finally—silence.

Esteban exhaled through his nose, nodding once. "We move. Now."

They didn't argue.

Adrenaline surged through Sylvie's veins as they pressed forward, moving faster now, ignoring the fire in their legs, the burning in their lungs. Muskcobar was right beside him, his breaths coming quick and sharp, but he kept pace.

And then, suddenly—

The trees began to thin.

Sylvie felt the change before she saw it. The thick shadows of the jungle gave way to something brighter. Sunlight. The sky opened up, vast and blue, the oppressive canopy of leaves breaking apart above them.

Ahead, the dense greenery parted, revealing open terrain—rolling hills, a dirt road in the distance, civilization just beyond reach.

Esteban turned to them; his expression unreadable. "We made it."

Muskcobar let out a triumphant laugh, throwing an arm around Sylvie's shoulders. "See? Easy."

Sylvie shoved him off, too exhausted to argue. Her legs trembled beneath her, but she forced herself to stay upright. The jungle was behind them.

But somehow, she knew—the hardest part was still ahead.

18 | PANAMA PAPERS

The air in Panama City clings to the skin like a damp shroud, thick with the mingling scents of saltwater, exhaust fumes, and sweat. The city pulses with energy—glass skyscrapers reflecting the blinding sun, casting sharp shadows over the bustling streets below. Banks, casinos, and luxury hotels line the avenues, symbols of both legitimate wealth and laundered fortunes.

Sylvie adjusts the brim of her hat, keeping his head low as he follows Muskcobar through the crowded sidewalks. Vendors peddle counterfeit watches and pirated electronics, their calls drowned out by the hum of traffic and the occasional honk of impatient drivers. Businessmen in tailored suits brush past, murmuring into Bluetooth headsets, their eyes fixed ahead as if the city's underbelly doesn't exist.

"This city reeks of stolen money," Sylvie mutters, adjusting the strap of her leather bag.

Muskcobar grins, unfazed. "That's why we're here, my love The kind of people who live in glass towers don't ask where the money comes from. They only ask how much."

Sylvie exhales sharply. Something about this place makes her skin crawl.

They turned onto a quieter street, where law firms and financial institutions stand shoulder to shoulder, the true heart of Panama's offshore empire. The sidewalks here are immaculate, the air thick with wealth and secrecy. No street vendors, no beggars—only tinted windows, security cameras, and men in suits who look like they carry more than just briefcases.

Muskcobar slows his stride, his gaze fixed on the gleaming white high-rise ahead. Its mirrored windows reflect the perfect blue sky, shielding whatever dealings go on inside. A brass plaque near the entrance glints in the sunlight and reads

GÓMEZ & ASSOCIATES—OFFSHORE SERVICES

Above a half torn brass plaque where the name "Mossack Fonseca" was barely readable

Sylvie stops just short of the entrance. "It's too clean," she murmured.

Muskcobar chuckles. "Of course, it is. No one trusts a dirty banker."

Sylvie scans the exterior. Something feels off. She knows better than to trust men like Felipe Gómez, but Muskcobar insists he's their best shot.

"We go in, we keep it short," Sylvie says. "No unnecessary details."

Muskcobar smirks, flicking the ash from his cigar. "Ah, Sylvie, you worry too much." "We get the money, we find your husband, I kill him and I marry you"

"Please no" "No what I do not get the money?

I do not kill him? or I do not marry you?"

She smiled "Please do not kill him".

He strides toward the entrance, pushing through the glass doors.

Inside, the marble floor gleams, reflecting the crystal chandelier hanging from the ceiling. The air-conditioning is set to an almost unnatural chill, a stark contrast to the suffocating heat outside. A massive abstract painting dominates the far wall—a meaningless swirl of colors meant to impress wealthy clients.

At the reception desk, a woman with sharp cheekbones and an even sharper gaze barely glances up from her screen. She wears a sleek headset, her manicured nails clicking against the keyboard.

Muskcobar leans in with his most charming smile. "We have an appointment."

She presses a button without looking up. A low beep sounds, and a deep voice crackles through the intercom.

"Send them in."

The heavy wooden doors at the end of the lobby unlock with a quiet click.

Muskcobar gestures toward them with a flourish. "After you, love."

Sylvie sighs. This is a mistake. She feels it in her gut.

But there's no turning back now. They step inside.

THE LAWYER

Eduardo Gómez sat behind a massive mahogany desk, the faint scent of leather and expensive cologne lingering in the air. His navy-blue suit was crisp, his gold Rolex peeking just beneath his tailored cuff, catching the light with every subtle movement. Everything about him spoke of wealth, power, and discretion.

A man who knew where the bodies were buried— because he had buried some of them himself.

He stood as they entered, flashing a polished smile. "Muskcobar. It's been too long."

"We need new identities. Bank accounts. A way to disappear."

Gómez chuckled; his amusement effortless. He sank back into his chair, fingers steepling. "Ah, the classic package." His sharp eyes flicked toward Muskcobar. "I assume you have cash?"

Muskcobar pulled a thick envelope from his jacket and tossed it onto the desk. "Half now. Half when the job is done."

Gómez picked up the envelope, weighing it in his palm as if he could judge its contents by feel alone. Satisfied, he nodded. "I can make you ghosts. But you'll need more than just fake names. You need cover—offshore companies, assets, a paper trail. You can't just stroll into Brazil or Argentina with a suitcase full of cash."

Sylvie crossed his arms, his unease growing. "How complicated is this?"

Gómez leaned back, the leather chair creaking softly. "Not at all. I've set up hundreds of these— real estate holdings, consulting firms, investment groups. The beauty of Panama is that no one asks too many questions."

Sylvie exchanged a glance with Muskcobar. Something about this felt too smooth, too effortless. But they were out of options.

Muskcobar smirked, tapping the desk lightly. "Do it."

THE ARREST

The paperwork took an hour. Passports, business registrations, financial trails leading to nowhere— Gómez worked with the precision of a man who had done this a thousand times. His fingers flew across the keyboard, numbers and identities shifting in real time as he rerouted ownership of shell corporations to their new aliases.

Sylvie watched, his unease growing. It was too easy.

Muskcobar, on the other hand, leaned back in his chair, completely at ease. "Smooth, Gómez. No wonder you're the best."

Gómez smirked, sliding the final documents across the desk. "And now, gentlemen, you're officially ghosts."

Then—the door burst open.

The crack of wood against metal made Sylvie's stomach drop before his brain could process what was happening.

Federal agents. Guns drawn. Shouting. Chaos.

Gómez's face drained of color as the room flooded with officers in tactical gear. His hands shot into the air, panic flashing in his eyes. "This is a mistake!" he stammered.

Sylvie barely had time to react before he felt Muskcobar' s grip on his arm—strong, urgent.

"We need to go. Now."

Gómez let out a strangled noise as an officer slammed him against the desk, wrenching his arms behind his back. Papers scattered. The hard drive hit the floor.

"Eduardo Gómez, you're under arrest for financial fraud, money laundering, and conspiracy."

Gómez turned to them, his face pale, his voice barely above a whisper. "Run."

Muskcobar didn't need to be told twice.

Sylvie hesitated—a split second of indecision. Then she moved. Fast.

They shoved past stunned employees, bodies blurring around them as they sprinted down the corridor.

The emergency exit was ahead.

Then—sirens.

Sylvie's pulse hammered. Outside, flashing lights bathed the streets in red and blue. The noose was tightening.

Panama was no longer safe.

19 | SUBMARINE

THE ESCAPE BEGINS

The moment Sylvie and Muskcobar hit the alley behind Gómez's office, the city erupts. Sirens wail through the humid night, bouncing off the high-rise buildings. The chaos of flashing lights and shouting officer's spills into the streets.

Sylvie's heart slams against his ribs as he scans their surroundings. They're running blind.

Muskcobar grabs his arm. "Come on, we move!"

Sylvie yanks himself free. "Move where? They have roadblocks everywhere!" Muskcobar smirks, his breath steady despite the madness unfolding around them. "Then we don't take the roads."

Before Sylvie can argue, Muskcobar is already dialing a number on his burner phone. He mutters something rapid and urgent in Spanish before ending the call.

"Our ride is waiting at the docks."

Sylvie doesn't like the sound of that. He's been in the game long enough to know that when Muskcobar has a 'ride' planned, it's never straightforward. But they have no choice. The streets are crawling with law enforcement.

They sprint toward the old district, weaving through alleys, dodging vendor stalls and street carts. A news bulletin blares from a café's television.

Breaking News: Prominent Panama Lawyer Eduardo Gómez Arrested for Money Laundering— International Investigations Underway.

Muskcobar doesn't slow down. "They're already spinning the story."

Sylvie grits his teeth. "How long before our faces are plastered all over that screen?"

Muskcobar glances at his watch. "I'd say about... ten minutes?"

Sylvie cursed under her breath" I hope they have a decent picture of me"

Ahead, the neon glow of the docks flickers through the fog rolling in from the bay. The smell of saltwater and diesel fuel fills the air. They cut through an old boatyard where half-sunken trawlers rust away, forgotten by time.

Muskcobar finally stops behind a row of cargo containers. "We wait here."

Sylvie wipes sweat from his forehead. "For what?"

Muskcobar just grins. "You'll see."

A low rumble vibrates beneath their feet.

Sylvie turns, expecting a speedboat or a small freighter. Instead, an old, battered submarine rises from the water like a mechanical beast from a forgotten war.

Sylvie blinks. "Tell me this is a joke."

A man in a Hawaiian shirt lean against the sub, cigar clenched between his teeth. He tilts his sunglasses down and smirks.

"Always full of surprises, hermano," the man says.

Muskcobar claps him on the back. "Juan, mi viejo amigo. Still running this thing?"

Juan exhales a long stream of smoke. "Still regretting every deal I ever made with you."

Sylvie shakes his head. "We're not actually getting in that thing, are we?"

Muskcobar pats the submarine like it's an old dog. "Unless you want to take your chances with the coast guard?"

Sylvie glances back at the streets behind them. Flashlights bob in the distance. The net is closing in.

She sighs. "Fine. But if I die in this rust bucket, I'm haunting you."

Juan gestures toward the hatch. "Then welcome aboard the Sancho Panza."

DIVING INTO DANGER

Inside, the submarine is worse than Sylvie feared. The walls are lined with rust, streaked from years of salt exposure. The cramped interior is dimly lit by flickering overhead lights, their faint buzzing adding to the suffocating silence. The air is thick with the pungent smell of oil, metal, and sweat— each breath feels like inhaling the inside of an old machine.

Sylvie ducks his head, maneuvering into the narrow corridor as the steel hatch above slams shut with a dull thunk. The sound reverberates through the hull, a metallic finality that settles like lead in his gut. The weight of it all—the escape, the uncertainty, the sheer insanity of trusting Muskcobar's plan— presses down on him.

Juan twists the hatch's locking wheel until it won't budge. "Alright, señores, make yourselves comfortable." He grins, wiping his greasy hands on his already stained shirt. "Next stop: anywhere but here."

Sylvie glances at Muskcobar, who has already made himself at home, lounging against a wall like he's on a luxury yacht instead of a half-sunken relic.

"Juan, I assume we're running silent?" Muskcobar asks, voice as casual as if he were ordering another round of drinks.

Juan flips a row of switches overhead. The submarine hums in response, vibrating slightly as its engines engage. "You assume correctly." He adjusts a dial, and the sound drops into a muffled whisper, the steady hum now nearly imperceptible. "But just because we're underwater doesn't mean we're invisible."

Sylvie frowns. "What does that mean?"

Juan jerks his thumb toward a flickering radar screen mounted on the control panel. Green waves sweep across the display, forming ghostly outlines of nearby obstacles. "It means the Panamanian coast guard is paranoid as hell. They sweep these waters constantly. And trust me, if they pick us up, they won't be calling for backup."

Muskcobar leans back, exhaling through his nose. "I have a lot of friends among the politicians in the Caribbean. We do business together." He flashes a grin. "If we reach the right island, we'll be safe."

Sylvie scoffs. "And if we don't reach the right island?"

Juan flicks another switch, dimming the cabin lights. The submarine's interior is bathed in a dull red glow, making everything feel even more claustrophobic. He turns to Sylvie, expression unreadable. "Then I hope you know how to swim."

The hum of the engines fades into the background. Water sloshes against the hull, deep and endless, as they slip further beneath the waves. Sylvie lets out a slow breath, her fingers gripping the armrests of her seat. She has never feared water, but this—this is different.

She has spent his life in kitchens, working in heat, surrounded by fire. Air has always been plentiful. But here, buried in the belly of a rusted beast, surrounded by thousands of tons of crushing pressure, there is no air. There is no escape.

Muskcobar, as always, looks unbothered. He tilts his head back against the cold steel wall, his cigar tucked behind his ear. "Relax, Sylvie. You're acting like we haven't survived worse."

The submarine lurched violently to the side, the metal hull groaning under pressure. Water dripped from the ceiling as alarms blared, casting an eerie red glow over the cramped interior. Pablo struggled to regain his footing, gripping onto the nearest handrail while Sylvie, her face pale but defiant, pressed herself against the control panel.

Outside, the dark ocean pressed against them, an unforgiving abyss stretching in every direction. Sonar pings echoed through the vessel, each one a reminder that the authorities were closing in.

"This is not how I imagined our honeymoon," Muskcobar muttered. "We were supposed to be in a five-star resort, sipping mojitos."

Sylvie exhaled sharply, wiping a strand of damp hair from her face. "I've never drowned before. So yes, this feels considerably worse."

He shot her a glance, a grim smirk tugging at the corner of his lips. "I promised adventure, didn't I?"

She rolled her eyes. "I was thinking cocktails on the beach, not evading international law enforcement in a tin can."

A sudden explosion rattled the submarine. The sonar pings grew faster, closer. Juan swore under his breath, gripping the wheel as the vessel tilted again. Bubbles rose past the porthole—depth charges.

"They're trying to flush us out," Sylvie whispered, her fingers tightening around the edge of the console.

"No kidding," Juan growled. "Hold on."

With a flick of a switch, the submarine nosedived into the abyss, leaving behind the chaotic echoes of the chase. The ocean swallowed them whole, darkness consuming everything except the flickering emergency lights inside the vessel.

Sylvie let out a slow breath. "So, how do we get out of this one?"

Muskcobar hesitated, then grinned. "I was hoping Juan had a plan."

Juan smirks, his hands gliding over the controls with the ease of a man who has lived more time underwater than on land. "First time for everything, amigo."

Sylvie shoots him a glare. "That is not comforting."

Juan chuckles, keeping his eyes on the instruments. "Just keep breathing. That's all you have to do."

Sylvie closes her eyes for a moment, steadying himself. Breathe. Just breathe.

The walls of the submarine seem to tighten around him, the metal groaning softly as they sink deeper into the abyss.

THE CHASE BEGINS

For the first hour, the submarine glides through the depths like a ghost. The ocean around them is vast and silent, their presence undetected. Sylvie keeps his gaze fixed on the dim red lights of the control panel, listening to the steady hum of the engines.

Muskcobar leans back, arms crossed, looking utterly at ease. "See? Smooth sailing."

Sylvie doesn't respond. She doesn't trust smooth. Smooth never lasts.

And then—an alarm blare.

Juan curses under his breath, his hands flying over the controls. The radar screen flickers, bright green dots appearing where before there was only empty ocean. His jaw tightens. "Coast guard patrol. Fast."

Sylvie's stomach knots. "How close?"

Juan exhales sharply. "Close enough to ruin our night."

Muskcobar barely reacts. He takes his cigar from behind his ear and lights it with a practiced flick of his lighter. The glow briefly illuminates his face before he exhales a slow plume of smoke. "So, we go deeper."

Juan spins in his chair, leveling Muskobar with a glare. "We can't. This thing wasn't built for deep dives. If we push too far, we'll end up crushed like a tin can." "Please do not smoke"

A sudden ping echoes through the hull. A second later, another.

Sylvie stiffens. "What was that?"

Juan's face darkens. "Sonar. They're looking for us."

Sylvie grips the metal armrests of his seat. "And if they find us?"

Juan doesn't answer immediately. He watches the radar, lips pressing into a thin line. Finally, he mutters, "Then we get to see how good their depth charges are."

Muskcobar exhales another cloud of smoke. "Not a fan of that option."

Sylvie clenches his jaw. "We need a way out."

Muskcobar grins, leaning forward. "We need a distraction."

Juan snorts. "Oh, sure. Let me just pull a magic trick out of my ass."

Muskcobar taps the console. "Can we launch anything?"

Juan pauses, then smirks. "You want fireworks?" He flips a switch. "I can give you fireworks."

A loud clank reverberates through the submarine as an emergency flare torpedo ejects toward the surface. It ascends rapidly, slicing through the dark water like a signal to the gods.

Juan watches the radar, his fingers drumming against the console. "Come on… take the bait…"

Seconds stretch into eternity.

Then, the blip representing the coast guard ship begins to veer.

Juan grins. "They're buying it… for now."

Muskcobar chuckles. "See, love? Nothing to worry about."

Sylvie doesn't relax. Not yet.

THE SEARCH FOR SANCTUARY

Hours pass, and the submarine surfaces near a chain of small islands. The air is warm, the sea calm, but the tension is thick.

Juan scans the horizon, eyes narrowing. "We need a place to dock."

Muskcobar leans over his shoulder, his grin unmistakable. "I've got contacts. Dominican Republic, St. Kitts, maybe even Cuba."

Sylvie arches an eyebrow, skeptical. "Maybe?"

Muskcobar chuckles lowly, adjusting his stance. "A few deals, a few... favors. Let's just say some presidents owe me." His tone is teasing, but there's an edge to it.

Sylvie crosses his arms, staring out at the water. "That's comforting," she mutters, his voice dripping with sarcasm.

Juan keeps his eyes on the water, but his voice is steady. "We go in fast. No lights. We get caught; you better pray they're friendly."

Sylvie exhales sharply, rubbing his face. "This was supposed to be a simple escape." His words hang in the air, filled with regret.

Muskcobar slaps him on the back, a booming laugh escaping him. "When have we ever done simple?" He glances at Sylvie, his eyes sparkling with mischief. "You should know by now, nothing worth doing is ever easy."

Juan turns the wheel, guiding the submarine toward a quiet cove. "Stay sharp," he warns, his voice low. "If someone's waiting for us, it's too late to back out now."

Sylvie clenches his jaw, watching the shoreline grow closer in the dim light. Her stomach churns, but he doesn't dare look away.

"This is the part I hate," she mutters, half to herself.

Muskcobar leans back, clearly enjoying the moment. "Landing's always the hardest. That's where the real fun starts."

As the submarine drifts toward land, Sylvie feels the weight of it all. The hardest part isn't just the landing—it's what comes next.

Something in his gut tells her their troubles are just beginning.

20 | HAITI

ARRIVAL IN HAITI

The submarine drifts silently toward the Haitian coastline, its dark silhouette barely visible against the restless sea. The waves slap rhythmically against the hull, a steady reminder of the vast ocean they've just crossed. Overhead, the sky is a deep, impenetrable black, dotted with faint stars, their glow barely enough to pierce the oppressive night.

Muskcobar, gripping the controls, cuts the engine with a quiet click. The mechanical hum dies, leaving only the sound of water lapping against metal. The absence of noise feels deafening. The air inside the submarine is thick with tension and salt, sweat clinging to their skin. For a long moment, neither man speaks.

Sylvie rises from her seat and steps onto the deck. A gust of humid air wraps around him, thick and suffocating. He inhales deeply, tasting the briny wind mixed with the faint scent of burning wood from distant shorelines. The jagged outline of Haiti stretches across the horizon, flickering village lights dotting the coast like fireflies in the darkness.

"Haiti," she mutters, her voice barely above a whisper. "Not exactly the plan."

Muskcobar stretches his arms behind his head, rolling his shoulders with a lazy grin. "Better than a torpedo up our asses," he remarks, his voice tinged with amusement.

Sylvie doesn't share his enthusiasm. She studies the shoreline, his eyes scanning for movement. She knows Haiti. She's been here before—under different circumstances. This land is alive, pulsing with a rhythm of its own. It breathes danger and opportunity in equal measure. And tonight, as fugitives, they're stepping into it blind.

"We need to find a place to lay low," Sylvie says, her tone all business. "Somewhere we won't stand out."

Muskcobar chuckles, the sound dry and knowing. "Two tourists fresh off a submarine? Oh yeah, we'll blend right in."

Sylvie ignores him, her eyes fixed on the darkened terrain ahead. "Port-au-Prince is too risky. Too many eyes. Too many questions." She exhales slowly, calculating. "We head for the Tortuguero A small village. Somewhere we can regroup and get our bearings."

Muskcobar nods, his expression sobering. "We go in quiet, stay off the main roads. If we're lucky, we find transport before sunrise."

Sylvie doesn't respond immediately. She watches as a shadow moves among the distant trees. It could be an animal. It could be something worse. Either way, they have no choice but to go ashore.

DISEMBARKING UNDER THE COVER OF DARKNESS

The submarine's small hatch creaks open as Muskcobar retrieves an inflatable raft, tossing it overboard. It hits the water with a soft splash, barely audible over the whispering waves. Sylvie climbs down first, his boots landing in the shallow vessel. He steadies himself, gripping the paddle tightly. Muskcobar follows, pushing off from the submarine's side, sending them drifting toward shore.

The warm saltwater laps at the raft's edges as they move in near silence, each paddle stroke careful and deliberate. Sylvie's grip tightens, his knuckles white. Every splash sound too loud. Every movement feels like an invitation for disaster. The jungle-lined beach ahead is both a refuge and a snare, its darkened outline concealing whatever awaits them.

Muskcobar is the first to jump out as the raft scrapes against the sand. His boots sink into the wet shore, the scent of salt and damp vegetation surrounding him. He straightens, scanning the area with sharp eyes before nodding. "Clear."

Sylvie follows, his muscles tense. They drag the raft up the beach, shoving it into the thick underbrush where it disappears beneath tangled vines. The air is thick with humidity, the scent of earth and decay clinging to their skin. Crickets and unseen creatures sing a haunting nocturnal melody. Somewhere in the distance, a drumbeat echoes— faint, steady, almost hypnotic.

Sylvie stiffens. Drums. They could mean celebration. They could mean warning.

"We need to move," she says quietly. "Sunrise isn't far."

Muskcobar pulls out a small flashlight, shielding the beam with his hand as he consults a crumpled map. His brows furrow in concentration. "There's a village a few kilometers inland. If we keep to the jungle, we should be able to avoid any unwanted attention."

Sylvie nods, his jaw tight. He adjusts the strap of his pack, exhaling slowly. The hardest part of any journey is always the landing.

And something tells him their troubles are only just beginning.

A TENSE JOURNEY INLAND

They push forward, cutting through the thick foliage. The jungle is alive around them, the rustling leaves whispering secrets. Sylvie keeps his eyes sharp, ears tuned to every unnatural sound. Years of survival instincts scream at her to stay on edge.

"You hear that?" Muskcobar whispers, stopping in his tracks.

A rustling ahead. Not the wind. Something deliberate.

Sylvie motions for silence. They crouch, gripping their weapons. The underbrush shifts, and a shadow emerges—a gaunt man in ragged clothes, a machete hanging loosely at his side. His dark eyes flick between them, wary but not immediately hostile.

"Travelers?" the man asks in Creole.

Sylvie nods cautiously. "on cherche ou dormir, where to sleep."

The man studies them for a moment, then jerks his head toward the path. "Venez pani problems Come. Before less gangsters finds you."

Muskcobar and Sylvie exchange wary glances before following him into the trees. Sylvie isn't sure if they're being saved or led into a new kind of danger.

THE AMBUSH

They take a small inflatable raft to shore, paddling in silence. The ocean stretches behind them, a vast, black void swallowing every sound but the rhythmic splash of their paddles. The salt air is thick, heavy with moisture, clinging to their skin. The shore looms closer, a thin strip of sand bordered by tangled jungle. No lights, no movement—just the whisper of waves licking the beach.

Sylvie is the first to jump out, boots sinking into the wet sand. She grips the raft and hauls it onto the shore, his eyes darting across the tree line. Muskcobar steps beside him, scanning the darkness.

The night is too quiet.

Then—

A distant whistle slices through the humid air. Sharp. Purposeful.

Sylvie freezes, every muscle locking in place. His breath catches in his throat.

Another whistle. Closer this time.

His pulse quickens. He recognizes the sound. A call. A signal.

"Did you hear that?" Sylvie mutters, barely above a whisper.

Muskcobar nods, his hand instinctively moving toward his waistband. "Yeah. And I don't like it."

Sylvie keeps his voice low. "We need to move. Now."

They push inland, slipping into the shadows of towering palms and thick underbrush. Twigs snap beneath their boots. The humidity clings to them, sweat forming on their brows. The jungle is alive with the distant chirp of insects and rustling leaves. But something feels... off.

The whistles come again. This time from multiple directions.

A chill creeps down Sylvie's spine. They're being tracked.

Then—flashlights.

Dozens of them.

The beams cut through the dense foliage, bobbing like fireflies in the dark. Shadows twist and flicker. The light catches the glint of metal—rifles.

"Down!" Muskcobar hisses, yanking his gun free.

Too late.

Figures emerge from the jungle, moving like wraiths, their faces masked by darkness. More flashlights flick on, casting an eerie glow over the sand. Sylvie's fingers twitch toward his belt, but he stops himself. He's outnumbered. He knows when a fight is unwinnable.

A tall man steps forward, the light catching the deep scars that slash across his face. He wears a loose tactical vest, his fingers drumming lazily against an AK-47 slung across his chest. The jungle behind him shifts with movement—more men, their eyes predatory, their weapons at the ready.

The man tilts his head, his lips curling into a grin.

"Well, well," he drawls, his voice smooth but edged with something dangerous. "Look what the tide dragged in."

Sylvie's stomach tightens. That voice.

He hasn't heard it in years.

"Fete Nationale" She mutters.

The man's grin widens. "Ahh, so you do remember me." He spreads his arms in mock welcome. "I was beginning to think you forgot."

Muskcobar raises an eyebrow. "Fete Nationale, that's your name?"

The warlord chuckles, the sound low and rough. "To my friends." His expression hardens, smile vanishing. "To my enemies? Death."

Sylvie doesn't move, doesn't blink. She knows what Fete Nationale is capable of.

One of Fete Nationale men steps forward, gripping Muskcobar' s shoulder. Muskcobar shoves him off, but another rifle barrel presses into his spine.

More men close in. Rough hands grab Sylvie, shoving her forward. She jerked away, but a rifle butt slams into her ribs. Pain explodes through her side, stealing his breath. she stumblec, gasping.

Muskcobar snarls as they wrestle him down. "You're making a mistake."

Fete Nationale crouches in front of Sylvie, studying him like a predator sizing up wounded prey. His dark eyes gleam in the dim light.

"No, mon ami," he says softly, his accent thick. "You made the mistake. Stepping onto my island uninvited."

Sylvie clenches his jaw. She knows Fete Nationale well enough to recognize that look in his eyes. Amusement laced with cruelty. A cat toying with a trapped mouse.

The men forced Sylvie and Muskcobar toward an old, rusted truck parked just beyond the trees. The doors groan as they are shoved inside, their hands roughly bound.

The engine roars to life, choking out a cloud of black smoke as the tires dig into the dirt. The jungle blurs past as they speed into the Haitian night, swallowed by the darkness.

Sylvie shifts, testing his restraints, but the ropes are tight—too tight.

Muskcobar exhales sharply. "Any brilliant escape plans?"

Sylvie remains silent, eyes locked on the darkened road ahead.

Because deep in his gut, she knew —wherever they're going, it's worse than here.

CAPTIVITY

Hours later, the dim light of the warehouse flickers weakly above them, casting long shadows on the cracked dirt floor. The air is suffocating, thick with the acrid stench of oil, sweat, and blood. Sylvie can feel the heat of it seeping into his skin, settling in his bones. Hrt hands are bound tightly behind her, and every subtle movement sends sharp pains up her arms.

Muskobar leans back against the wall, his gaze never leaving the man sitting across from him. Fete Nationale, the grinning bastard, spins a knife between his fingers like it's a casual hobby. His smirk never falters.

Sylive pledged with Fete Nationale "We were friends before I made you the chef of the White House. I remember your chicken Voodoo; my husband made you president of Haiti"

"Now," Fete Nationale says, voice low and mocking, "is he willing to pay for your sorry asses?" "I understand he left America in a hurry, broke and a wanted fugitive"

Muskcobar arches an eyebrow, unbothered by the taunt. "Do You take crypto?"

Fete Nationale yes narrow, unimpressed. He stops spinning the knife and slides it into its sheath with a deliberate, slow motion. "You think this is a joke?"

Sylvie exhaled, the breath coming out in a sharp hiss. "You're smarter than this. You know who is my Colombian friend." Her voice is steady, measured, though her mind races. Muskcobar needs to get out of here he needs to keep them both alive.

Fete Nationale pauses, his grin faltering for just a second. He crouches down in front of Muskcobar, eyes narrowing as he sizes him up, calculating. After a moment, he leans in, his face inches from Muskcobar, and grins that wide, unsettling grin. "I do. That's why I know someone will pay to get you back."

The door to the warehouse slams open, and the sound of boots hitting the floor rings through the space, followed by the unmistakable shriek of metal. A group of heavily armed fighters' storm in, weapons raised, eyes scanning the room with deadly precision.

"They have arrived" let's go to the helicopters

Dressed in street clothes, Jean Pierre and his team stepped ashore and headed to a modest Lambi restaurant a few miles from where was Fete Nationale and his thugs

Lucio glanced around and whispered, "Hide in the kitchen and make us some special cookies, here is some Brugmansia."

The Haitian staff didn't question it. Jean Pierre took over the humble kitchen, improvising with the limited ingredients. Hours later, three helicopters appeared on the horizon, landing nearby. Emerging from one was Fête Nationale, the former White House chef turned Haitian president called Uncle Doc—and the island's most powerful narco. He had gained weight since becoming president and started to look like Amin Dada the defund president and dictator of Uganda. His country was always a human drama, while the top-ranking politicians of Haiti were buying properties in Paris and Geneva when fortunate and shot by gangsters when unlucky.

Fête Nationale and his lieutenants sauntered over to Lucio, gun at his side. "I hear you brought me snow in that sub."

Lucio smiled. "I did. Let's have coffee and cookies."

A server brought the tray. Lucio pushed it toward Fête, who rested his pistol on the table.

"You first," Fête said, his gaze icy.

Lucio took a sip of coffee and bit into a cookie. "We need to talk. Just us. Our men can wait outside."

Fête nodded, gesturing for his guards to step away. Both sides lingered near the entrance, eyes locked, fingers twitching near triggers.

Fête bit into a cookie. His eyes widened. "These are out of this world. Reminds me of a French chef I knew. Tastes just like his." He reached for another, indulgence melting his stern facade. He indulged and finished all the cookies.

But soon his hands trembled. Sweat beaded on his brow. His vision blurred.

Jean Pierre emerged from the kitchen, wiping his hands on a towel. "Funny seeing you again, Fête. Crook, Extortionist, Thief. Drug trafficker." His voice dropped. "My cookies are better than your chicken voodoo. I added a little Quimbois. Some "Devil's Breath" You're going to sleep."

As Fête's head drooped, Jean Pierre hummed softly. "Duerme Negrito," the haunting lullaby of Atahualpa Yupanqui.

Lucio leaned closer, smirking. "You picked the biggest cookie. Bad call. I ate the small one."

With effort, they dragged Fête back to the submarine. Meanwhile, Lucio's men discreetly handed wads of cash to Fête's bodyguards.

One guard chuckled, tucking the bills away. "We change presidents every six months. We do prefer the money."

"We have two prisoners at the moment a French woman and a Colombian guy for another $500 we let them go, if that works for you"

Lucio did not hesitate "please do tell them to cross to the Dominican Republic and go to the US Embassy" here is my business card.

22 | LATIN FIANCEE VISA

O ne week later in Miami, celebrations erupted. The arrest of Fête Nationale for smuggling tons of cocaine into the U.S. dominated the headlines. Jean Pierre, Sandra, and Lucio stood alongside the mayor, receiving praise from the Haitian diaspora—along with an unexpected nod from Trump himself.

"This is a great achievement by the DEA and Agent Lucio," the mayor announced. "We also appreciate the cooperation of Chef Jean Pierre and his friend Sandra. They will share the bounty on his head, which is…" He paused, fumbling with his papers as an aide whispered in his ear. His eyes widened. "A substantial sum," he added with a grin. "And Miss Sandra, you have been granted immunity and Fiancée visa.

The Mayor took Jean Pierre apart "Donald Trump want a word with you" and he handed him his phone.

"Jean Pierre, you are a French cook, an ex-president, a foreign political adviser, and now a bounty hunter—this is huge! This is what America needs." He added

"Are you alone?"

"Yes, Donald. If the phone isn't tapped."

"I need your help?"

"My help? For sure you have a dinner party?"

"Sort of, but I am the piece de resistance"

"They want me to be replaced?"

"Who?"

"Congress, The Democrats, The Supreme Court, Elon."

I know you've been there before. Believe me, I do not want to be replaced."

"Is that fake news?" Jean Pierre asked.

"No. They don't want me to drain the swamp—they want to trade me."

"By who?"

"By artificial intelligence."

"Witch hunt. Total disaster."

"Can we meet? You and your lovely fiancée. I'll bring Ivana—sorry, Melania. I need your political experience as much as your food"

"Sans problème. With pleasure."

"Your restaurant next week. I alone cannot fix it."

He hung up.

Jean Pierre returned to his kitchen in New York, immersing himself in the rhythmic dance of chopping, searing, and plating. The restaurant, his sanctuary, bustled with life as the weeks rolled by. Each day, the rich aroma of garlic and rosemary wafted through the air, mingling with the soft hum of conversation and clinking glasses.

The kitchen was where he belonged. The soft glow of candlelight on the tables and the laughter of satisfied patrons became the soundtrack to his evenings. But as successful as the restaurant became, there was a shadow that lingered in his mind — the faint outline of Sylvie.

It was a chilly Thursday evening when the past stepped into his present. The doorbell chimed, and there she stood. Sylvie, her once vibrant face pale and drawn, eyes heavy with regret. Jean Pierre paused, wiping his hands on his apron, before stepping out from behind the counter.

"Jean Pierre," she began, her voice trembling. "I made mistakes." "Larry had muscles but no brain" "Muskcobar is no good he made me walk the Dorian passage, travel in a submarine and escape from Haiti to Santo Domingo, he told me he wants to kill you and get younger women"

The words hung in the air like steam from a simmering pot. "You're the man for me" "I realized I Love you "She whispered, her eyes pleading.

Jean Pierre's gaze drifted past Sylvie to the far side of the room, where Sandra stood by the entrance, greeting guests. Her dark hair shimmered under the soft lights, and her warm smile lit the room like the first rays of dawn.

He met Sylvie's eyes, offering her a gentle, yet firm smile. "I'm sorry," he said softly, his accent curling around each word. "I'm just a French loser for you and a French lover for her, I am divorcing you, you remember Sandra" He glanced at Sandra, whose laughter filled the space between them like music.

"She is my Latin fiancée."